Praise for *Out of the Shadow*

Garfield's personal and com... ...*aught*
nuances of family dynamics, s... ...*d the*
power of control over a youn... ...*f the*
child who is often forgotten in ...*...other. A must-read*
for teenagers and parents!

— ESTHER FROGEL, PH.D.
LICENSED PSYCHOLOGIST

≈

Providing an enriching behind-the-closed-door view into what takes place in therapy, Out of the Shadow *leaves a lasting and uplifting impact. It is a gripping page-turner, full of fascinating wisdom that is illuminated in a stirring and delightfully absorbable way. This book authentically demonstrates how stagnant and even painful family relationships can be healed. The riveting story unfolds in a way that not only offers hope but a clear path to a more joyful way of living, through gently removing the blockages that allow each soul to shine. Priceless!*

— BRACHA GOETZ
HARVARD-EDUCATED RESEARCHER ON ANOREXIA
AUTHOR, *SEARCHING FOR GOD IN THE GARBAGE*

≈

Out of the Shadow's *captivating characters give an inspiring, relatable, and honest voice to the challenges and triumphs of the therapy process.*

— AARON FELDMAN, PH.D.
LICENSED PSYCHOLOGIST

OUT OF THE SHADOW

A Novel

Rochelle Garfield

ISBN: 978-965-7041-12-3 (paperback)
ISBN: 978-965-7041-13-0 (ebook)

Publishing services provided by JewishSelfPublishing. The author acts as publisher and is solely responsible for the content of this book, which does not necessarily reflect the opinions of JewishSelfPublishing.

www.jewishselfpublishing.com
info@jewishselfpublishing.com
(800) 613-9430

The author can be contacted at
rochellegarfieldauthor@gmail.com.

We sincerely hope you enjoy reading this book. The author would be very gratified if you would show your support by posting a nice review on Amazon.

≈

This book is dedicated in loving memory of my grandmother, Ethel Bagry Shafran. Her legendary and extraordinary love of creativity sparked my interest in writing from a very young age. Her constant positive feedback, encouragement, and belief in me gave me the courage to pursue my dream to write a novel.

≈

ACKNOWLEDGMENTS

First and foremost, I would like to thank my husband, Yerachmiel Garfield. His constant belief in me and endless encouragement to pursue my dreams has made all the difference. I feel so grateful to share the journey of life with him and so appreciative for his endless support for all my passions.

I would like to thank my parents, Rabbi Simcha and Esky Cook, for helping me believe in myself from the time I was a baby. They always acted amazed by whatever I did and made me believe I could reach for the stars. My mother was, and is, the best role model for pursuing creative passions and for always using her talents to make people happy.

I would like to thank my in-laws, Norman and Linda Garfield, for reading everything I write, giving me great feedback, and always encouraging me to go for my dreams. My mother-in-law has taught me by amazing example that it's never too late to develop your talents and passions and how rewarding it is to live a life immersed in creativity.

I have tremendous appreciation for Mrs. Tova Salb for her remarkable work editing the book, along with her encouragement to publish it.

I deeply appreciate Tamar Aumann Rosen for granting me an

extensive interview, sharing details from the Nobel Prize Ceremonies that she attended with her father, Professor Robert Aumann, recipient of the 2005 Nobel Prize in Economic Sciences. She gave me vital information and a personal account of what it was like to attend the ceremonies.

There are numerous people that helped and supported me along the way, and I am indebted to each one of them for their role in my life.

I want to thank my fifth-grade teacher, Lisa Shechter, who once told me that she thought I was a talented writer when I was only ten years old. I never forgot those words and the urge it created within me to want to keep writing.

I want to thank my eleventh-grade teacher, Reena Fohrman, for being a positive role model for me to pursue my dreams and do what I believe in, no matter what everyone else around me is doing.

I want to thank Mrs. Rochelle Goldberg for reading the book in its early stages and giving me invaluable feedback. I want to thank all my friends and family who read the book and whose positive feedback helped give me the courage to pursue publishing it.

Thank-you to Rabbi Eliyahu Miller for his vital role in making this project a reality, along with all of his encouragement and advice. And thank-you to Chaya Silverstone for her excellent, professional work in proofreading the final copy and catching the last errors.

Special appreciation to my awesome siblings and their spouses: Yeshaya and Milka Cook, Ephraim and Tova Cook, Sora Mindy and Dovid Cynamon, Tzirel and Yaakov Rutstein, and Velvel and Raizy Cook. Thank-you to Tzirel for always being such a great sounding board for all my ideas and thoughts.

Finally, I would like to thank my amazing children: Yaakov, Chaim, Ari, Talya, Shalom Uri, and Atara. They inspire me daily, each in their unique way. They are always a source of support and encouragement, and I feel so grateful for each of them. A special thank-you to Ari for his inimitable role in bringing this project to fruition.

Above all, I would like to express my tremendous appreciation to the Almighty for the endless gifts He has given me, including the ultimate gift of life and creativity — and for His help every step of the way.

PROLOGUE

WHEN THE SOUND OF A ringing phone jolted her awake at 4:47 a.m., Lori knew that something terrible had happened. Trembling, she groped about for the phone. With David snoring loudly beside her, and still half-asleep herself, she muttered a tense hello into the receiver.

Much to her surprise, she found herself mumbling congratulations. Her intuition had been dead wrong.

David rolled over. Having heard the congratulations, he asked who had a baby.

"No, no, no. It's not that at all. Much bigger news."

And then, for the second surprise that night, Lori found herself sobbing.

CHAPTER 1

ORI HAD A QUEASY FEELING in the pit of her stomach. And she didn't like it. Used to interacting with others in a confident and self-assured way, she was surprised at how anxious she was feeling. As she stepped out of her car into the crisp October air, a cool breeze rattled her already overstimulated brain. She breathed in deeply, trying to calm herself. *There is nothing to feel nervous about,* she reminded herself. After all, this was her element, the place where she was most successful.

Yes, but there's one significant difference, a little voice inside her piped up. *Today, the tables are turned.* This time, instead of empathizing, gently prodding, analyzing, and jotting notes, she'd be spilling her guts to a stranger who would be doing just that to her. Someone who'd read right through all her attempts at self-confidence, who'd know just how sad and insecure she really was.

Lori entered the office building and took the elevator up to the eighth floor as she contemplated the past few days. *This is not a big deal,* she tried to tell herself again and again. But the queasy feeling wouldn't go away. There was no escaping it.

She stepped into office 808 and walked up to the front desk, where a middle-aged woman with long, frizzy brown hair was sitting.

"I'm here to see Dr. Wilson," Lori stated briskly, trying to portray the air of coolness that she did not feel.

"Have a seat. He'll let you know when he's ready," the woman answered, without any hint of friendliness.

Lori took a seat on a worn-out tan couch with a few rips and tears in the lining. She picked up a random magazine from the glass coffee table in front of her, more to give herself something to hold than because she was actually interested in reading it. The office was shabbier then she had expected. Dr. Wilson had a stellar reputation; she'd thought he would have a more modern-looking place.

Lori quickly became lost in thought. What in the world was she thinking? Did she really need to do this? Why had she scheduled this appointment? She had analyzed her life many times over. She knew exactly why she acted, interacted, and reacted the way she did. She was a psychologist, for crying out loud. She didn't need anyone else's help. Lori gave a frustrated sigh. She knew that premise was irrational. Who didn't need help? And right now, she was desperate.

She could picture the scene as clear as if she were watching an instant replay in slow motion. The mom approaching her to discuss her daughter. The conversation beginning in a calm manner. And then her explosive, unprofessional rage directed at the mom. The mom storming away. Her daughter being pulled out of Lori's clinical program. Lori watching them as they walked out of her building. A sad, sad girl with big eyes that overwhelmed a skeletal body. Big eyes that had a desperate sort of stare. Begging for help. Being dragged away by a mom with small, slit-like eyes. Eyes of a tiger that had spotted its prey. Eyes that were bitter, angry, and threatening.

"Lori?"

She jumped slightly. Caught a little off guard, she quickly straightened up.

Dr. Wilson was standing over her, smiling gently. She stood up, smiling back, as she tried to appear self-assured. *Oh, what's the use?* she thought. *He'll know soon enough who I really am.*

"Good morning!" Dr. Wilson was looking deep into her eyes and Lori felt uncomfortable. She just couldn't shake this odd feeling of knowing he would be analyzing her inner motives. Invading her privacy. Is this how her own clients felt? As she looked back at him, she tried not to break eye contact.

Dr. Wilson was a little overweight and dressed surprisingly casual with an orange polo shirt and khaki pants. He looked to be in his early forties, although his thick head of hair helped give him a more youthful appearance.

"Good morning, Dr. Wilson. I really appreciate your giving me an appointment on such short notice." Lori's blond hair was pulled back in a ponytail. She was thin, wearing a tan cardigan, white oxford, and fitted pants. She suddenly felt like she was dressed too professionally, almost as if to make a point she didn't have to make.

"Hey, anything I can do. I really admire your work. I've read a lot of your research on eating disorders. I hear about you from many of my colleagues. I'm honored that you called me. And please, call me Ron." There was something warm and engaging about him. Something empathetic about his tone.

"Thanks." Lori smiled awkwardly.

"Well, come on back." Dr. Wilson motioned to Lori to follow him.

As she walked through the doors to the right of the secretary's window, Lori continued thinking back to what had brought her here. The final straw had been the phone call she had received three nights ago, and the powerful emotions it had unleashed within her. David had been urging her to seek therapy for years. It drove her crazy when he blamed some of her present actions on her past. Lori hated to admit that she needed help, but she did, so here she was. *Here goes nothing,* she thought.

Lori followed Dr. Wilson into his office. Glancing around, she saw a desk pushed off to the side, a couple of chairs and a couch in the center, and lots of interesting knickknacks lining the shelves of the wall.

"Please, have a seat." Dr. Wilson motioned to the chairs as he himself sat down on one of them.

Lori sat. An uncomfortable silence filled the air, until Dr. Wilson cleared his throat and said, "So what can I do for you?"

Lori had rehearsed this many times. "I am having some difficulty with countertransference with one of my clients. I also have an event coming up that's causing me significant and inappropriate emotional upheaval. These two situations have emphasized the fact that I haven't been successful in overcoming a part of my life I've been trying to avoid for many years. I need help probing into my past to help me understand my current life and relationships better."

Lori gave a nervous giggle, letting her guard down slightly. "I'm feeling quite nervous right now, and suddenly having a much greater appreciation for all my clients and what it must feel like for them to show up for an appointment. I really didn't think I'd feel this way. I have been in therapy before, though it was years ago." As Lori continued, she began feeling like she was rambling, her words tumbling out like a pile of clothes being dumped from a laundry bin.

"Look, as I said before, I'm honored that you called me. I don't have to tell you how well respected your work is, so believe me, I'm more nervous than you are!" Dr. Wilson said. "Rest assured, I'll pass no judgments. We're all human, as you and I know only too well. I like to say that our past and our follies only expound our successes."

"Thank you." Inwardly, Lori breathed a sigh of relief. He had left her dignity intact. "Well," she continued, "to make this all the more exciting, let me just add that I need to work this through in about two months' time."

"And the pressure mounts." Dr. Wilson sat back and laughed. The palpable tension in the room diminished somewhat. "You must have reasonable expectations, you know."

"Seriously, I know you're not going to remake me in two months, but I am hoping you can help me come to terms with at least *some* of my past in at least *some* functional way. I'm willing to come two or three times a week, if you have room in your schedule." Lori's voice had an almost pleading tone to it.

"Are you going to fill me in on what this two-month deadline is all about?"

"I...I'm...I'm sorry," Lori faltered uncharacteristically. "Do you mind if we don't talk about it yet? I can't totally explain it, but I'd prefer to wait to talk about it." She blushed. She knew why she didn't want to share this information. She wanted to share her past without being in her sister's shadow. She wanted that freedom for as long as she could push off discussing the inevitable.

Dr. Wilson turned his head ever so slightly. He was staring at Lori in a way that made her look away. "You do realize that this is interesting already?"

Lori closed her eyes briefly. "Yeah."

"Well then, where do you want to begin?"

"From the beginning, I guess."

"Sounds like a plan to me. So then, here's one of my favorite ways to start. Why don't you tell me about your earliest memory? I'm a firm believer that you always learn a lot from earliest memories."

Lori looked up as she thought a moment. "Interestingly, I think my first memory might be deceiving."

"From years of experience, I've become an adamant believer that first memories are rarely deceiving."

Lori shrugged. Then she began.

It was a hot summer day in July — one of those days when the air is thick with heat, and breathing in feels like you're sucking up steam. Sam and Elaine had decided to take their two girls to the pool for the afternoon. It was crowded there. The happy sounds of laughter and screaming wafted through the air, mingling with the steamy heat.

Sam and Elaine parked their belongings in a shady area under a tree. Elaine rummaged through the bag looking for sunscreen, while Sam spread out their towels.

Suddenly, out of the corner of her eye, Elaine glimpsed Lori running to the pool.

"Sam, grab Lori!"

Sam looked up. "Lori, come back!" he called as he headed toward her.

Lori was a precocious and fearless two-and-a-half-year-old. She loved the water.

Sam scooped her up. "Elaine, I'm going to take her in. Send Hannah when she has her sunscreen on."

Lori was moving about wildly in Sam's arms. It was evident that she was very excited to be there. "I want to go swimming, Daddy! I want to go swimming!"

"We're going, Lori! We're going." Sam laughed as he looked

at his daughter. Her charming blond curls were bouncing up and down.

Sam climbed into the pool first. "Okay, I'm ready."

Lori squeezed her eyes shut, as she always did before a jump. Then she leaped. She disappeared under the water, but only for a split second. She bobbed up and began to swim to her father, who was standing a few feet back.

"Wow!"

"How old is she?"

"Where did she learn to swim like that?"

People murmured around Sam. It was fun taking Lori swimming because people were always amazed that a child that young could swim like that.

Just then, Hannah came strolling down to the pool. She was six, with wavy brown hair and adorable dimples. Elaine came with her and climbed into the pool. Hannah sat down at the edge, but bent her legs back so even her toes did not reach the water.

"Hannah! Come in!" Elaine called, reaching out her hands to her.

"No." Hannah had a grimace on her face.

Elaine knew that look, but she persisted despite it. "Look at Lori. She's four years younger than you and she's swimming. If she can do it, so can you! Come on."

"No!" Hannah crossed her arms.

Sam passed Lori to Elaine. He reached out of the water and lifted Hannah to bring her into the pool.

Hannah began to shriek, squeezing her eyes shut, and shaking her head back and forth. "No, no, no, no, no!!"

"Calm down, Hannah." Sam tried to stay calm himself, but

Hannah was acting abnormal. With everyone in the pool watching, he began to turn red. He quickly put Hannah down. Then he turned to Elaine. "I tried, honey, but she's too stubborn."

Elaine responded, "We can't give up. She has to overcome this fear."

Sam shrugged.

So Hannah sat on the side the rest of the afternoon, while Lori swam precociously, delighting the crowds. She even jumped off the diving board.

"You're amazing, Lori! Do you know that?" Sam said as he wrapped Lori in a towel at the end of the day.

Those words stuck with her for a very long time.

Lori unclasped her hands, which she had been holding together tightly all the time she'd been speaking. All those details had come flooding back to her as she'd begun to speak. It felt like just yesterday.

Dr. Wilson interrupted her thoughts. "So let me guess. You and your sister have spent you lives vying for your parents' attention and adulation, competing for their love."

"Oh, you make it sound so mundane." Lori knitted her brow and chuckled.

"What more is life about than winning the admiration of the people you care most about?"

"Is that really what all of life boils down to?"

"Not all of life, but a very large portion."

"So then what happens if you lose?"

"I'll say what I always tell my sons when they play sports. It matters not who wins or loses, but how you play the game."

"I need time to process that. I'm not sure how you apply that to love and relationships." Lori's head was spinning even faster than it had been when she first came into the office.

"That's good timing, because our session was over a couple of minutes ago."

Lori looked down at her watch. Dr. Wilson was right. She looked up again. "Thank you. I think that was a good start."

"I agree. Although it'll be hard to remain in suspense, wondering what your deadline is all about."

Lori reached beside her for her purse. She slowly stood up. "See you next time!"

CHAPTER 2

Four Months Earlier

L ORI PARKED HER CAR IN one of the three spots marked "Director." She got out and strode briskly into the beautiful building looming before her. The clinic's grounds consisted of a three-story main building with mirrored walls, a sprawling campus with two additional buildings, and well-trimmed lawns decorated with lines of red and yellow tulips. It was an impressive sight by any standard.

Lori loved her work and tried not to take for granted how fortunate she was to have achieved her dream. Although she was walking fast, her mind was working in slow motion. Here before her was her baby, an amazingly successful eating disorder clinic that was building up an international reputation. She and two other partners — another psychologist and a psychiatrist — had begun the clinic as a small operation and it had grown into a successful enterprise.

It was strange, though. Lori, as successful as she was, would have imagined that at this point in life, she would be happy. All she wanted was happiness, once and for all. Plain and simple happiness. To be happy like a sunflower facing the sun, happy like a cloud floating peacefully above.

But happiness always seemed to be elusive. Just when she thought she had it firmly locked in her hands, it would slide through again. More often than not, Lori felt like a gray rain cloud filled with heaviness hanging in the air. That emptiness that ached inside her had diminished over the years, but it still poked its bitter head out from time to time. And many nights, she still found herself crying herself to sleep.

These feelings of sadness plagued her with guilt. How could she be so unhappy? And worse yet, what if the world realized? What if they knew that Lori Green, psychologist and renowned author/lecturer, had her own difficult relationships? What if they knew that Lori Green, healer of others, could not heal her own wounds?

She opened the glass doors and stepped inside the main building. She nodded hello to Elizabeth at the front desk. Elizabeth's shocking red hair always made Lori look twice, and Lori wondered if she would ever get used to it.

"How was your weekend, Elizabeth?"

"Fine. Neal was home, which was nice. How about yours?"

"Pretty relaxing. David had a gig and we all went to watch him." Lori was not in the mood for small talk, but she believed in being polite.

She continued through the doors to the left marked "Offices," and walked down the long corridor until she came to the office that read: "Dr. Lori Green, PhD, Director of Rainbow Eating Disorder Clinic." She opened the door and walked straight to her desk. She glanced up at the clock. Eight thirty-two. Right on time.

Lori sat down and let out her breath. Her desk was piled with folders of new and old patients. Her voice mail was blinking with new messages that she had to respond to. She turned on the computer, knowing there would be numerous emails to answer. Before she could even get overwhelmed, her phone started blinking. She glanced down and saw that the call was coming from Jessica, the therapist in charge of admissions.

"Good morning!" Lori picked up the phone, trying to sound cheerful.

"Good morning," Jessica responded matter-of-factly. Jessica had a stressful job, reading through applications and determining if patients were people that Rainbow Clinic could help. She was often dealing with crying, desperate parents. And she often had to say, "We're full at the moment," or "This isn't the place for your child." If she let her emotions into her job, Jessica wouldn't last a week. So it made sense that she kept her voice cold and businesslike.

"I just accepted a new client. She seems like a good fit for our clinic. She's been hospitalized two times and has seen a few therapists. Her case is severe, but I believe that we'll be able to help her. She lives in California. She'll be coming here with her mother. They've committed to staying for three months. I left her file on your desk. Her name is Allison something — I can't remember her last name. They should be arriving in two days."

"Thanks, Jessica. I'll read through her file and then determine her placement." Lori put the phone down and looked at the pile of folders. There, on the top, was a folder with the name Allison Maele on the cover.

At this point, Lori's main responsibilities in the clinic were reading through case files and assigning therapists to new patients, training all therapists in the Rainbow Clinic therapy technique, and overseeing and advising the therapists. She would treat up to five patients at a time herself, usually some of the more difficult cases. Lisa and Allen, the other two directors, had similar responsibilities. They split the entire caseload three ways; each oversaw a third of the patients.

Lori always enjoyed reading through new case files and determining which therapist would be best suited to see a new patient.

So here it was: Allison's file. Lori opened it and began to read.

≈

For most anorexics, it's hard to pinpoint exactly when the anorexia began. It often starts with a diet that slowly spirals out of control. But for Allison, it was not hard at all. She could identify the exact date that she became Anna, the secret name she called herself in her anorexic state. It was August 14, during the summer before her freshman year in high school. She remembered the date because it was two days before her fourteenth birthday. It was also the day that she had her wisdom teeth removed. That was the day that she stopped eating normally forever after. Or so she hoped. She never wanted to go back to the way she used to eat. Never, ever again. If only all her therapists would understand that. If only everyone would leave her alone…

She returned home from the oral surgeon with strict instructions not to eat any solids the rest of that day. Allison clearly remembered thinking that this might be a good way to jumpstart her diet. She wanted to lose some weight before the first day of school. She wanted to make a good impression. She wanted the girls to admire her. So she sucked on some ice cream and drank some juice. It felt good to go to bed a little hungry.

The next day, Allison thought she'd try eating only non-solid foods for another day. It wasn't so hard. She told her mother that her mouth was still hurting, and she ate only ice cream for a second day. The third day, Allison felt like she was on a roll. It got really hard not to eat a normal breakfast, but she felt great when she conquered her desire for solid food. For her birthday, Allison told her mom not to get her a cake because her mouth was still hurting. By the end of that week, Allison was thrilled to see that she had lost six pounds!

Her parents were slightly concerned and took her back to the oral surgeon to check if her mouth was okay. The oral surgeon confirmed that everything was healing just fine, and Allison should have no problem eating solids. That night, Allison's mother, Katie, demanded that she eat a real dinner. Allison panicked. She wasn't ready to eat solid food yet. She wanted to lose at least another ten pounds. But she had no more excuses. The oral surgeon had said everything was fine. So at dinner that night, she complained that her stomach was hurting and quickly went up to her room.

The next night at dinner, Allison's mother said that she could not leave the table until she ate at least some of the chicken salad. It had been Allison's favorite food. Allison felt like she was in turmoil. She absolutely could not eat the chicken; it would ruin her diet. But her mother was watching her with hawk eyes. So she took some chicken salad, and her mother breathed a sigh of relief. Allison cut it into pieces, pushed it around on her plate, and when her mother looked at her, she put a tiny piece in her mouth. When her mother looked away, she slipped a handful of the salad into her other hand, then reached behind her and quickly dumped it into the trash.

As soon as dinner was over, Allison rushed upstairs to her bathroom and weighed herself. Oh no! She had gained a pound. Why had she eaten that piece of chicken? Allison felt desperate. She went to her room, changed into her pajamas, and climbed into bed.

For some anorexics, the jump into anorexia is a slow and painful process. For Allison, it was fast and furious. Two weeks later, on the first day of school, Allison had lost fifteen pounds. She got the compliments that she had so looked forward to, her friends all jealously commenting on how "skinny" she looked. But ironically, although Allison enjoyed the comments, she suddenly felt like a loner. She didn't feel like hanging out with her friends. She stood with them, but felt like an observer. She felt like she had forgotten how to be part of a group. And worst of all, she felt like she had forgotten how to laugh.

When Allison's friends noticed that she wasn't eating, they began whispering among themselves. Finally, someone went to the school counselor, who called a meeting with Allison's mother. At the meeting, her mother reacted defensively and accused the counselor of falsely attributing disorders to her daughter without even having taken the time to talk to Allison. But as she walked out of the school building, she knew in her heart that her daughter was sick. Very sick.

The next day, Allison stayed home from school and went with her mother to her pediatrician. Allison was five feet four inches tall. At her last doctor's appointment three months earlier, she had weighed 118 pounds. Today, she weighed in at 97 pounds.

After the doctor met with two of them, he told Allison's mom that he wanted Allison in therapy immediately. He recommended a therapist and got her an appointment for that afternoon. Allison's heart was beating fast. She felt bad — like she was a horrible person. She felt guilty — like she was doing all this to get attention. She felt humiliated that she had a mental disorder. She just wanted to go home and lie under her warm blanket. She was cold and shivering and wanted to be *left alone*. And more than anything, she did not want anyone to make her eat anything. She wouldn't do it and no one could force her.

The therapist met with Allison, explained to her all about anorexia, and told her that she was going to help her get better. She told Allison that she had to gain two pounds by the next week. Then she told Allison's mother she had to make sure Allison ate 1,500 calories a day. Although that wasn't enough for Allison to get better, she would have to start slow, because her stomach was not used to eating solids and would have trouble digesting the food. Allison would have to eat everything in front of her mother or father, and they would check off the amount of calories she was eating on a chart.

Inside, Allison felt like exploding. No one — *no one* — would make her eat one thing more than she herself wanted to eat.

The week was torture. Allison did not go to school. She tried to stay in bed most of the time. Her mom or her dad, but mostly her mom, would bring food into her room and sit by her bed until she ate it. Her parents didn't realize it, but Allison was very good at slipping food into her pillowcase and then flushing it down the toilet after they had left her room.

At her next therapy appointment, both of Allison's parents came. Her dad was worried, too. They were both shocked when Allison was weighed in and had lost four more pounds. The therapist talked to her in front of her parents about hiding food. This week, the therapist suggested giving Allison milkshakes. It would be much harder to pretend to drink. Inside, Allison was boiling. This therapy was a joke! No one was helping her. And no one was going to make her eat.

That week, her parents switched off between cajoling and begging her to get her to eat, and screaming and threatening her to get her to eat. They tried coming up with punishments if she wouldn't drink the milkshakes, but nothing seemed to affect her. After Allison's mom left the room one night after two hours of cajoling, which only got her to drink half a milkshake,

Allison heard her go into her room and start throwing things at the wall. Allison buried her head deep in her blanket. She just wanted to die.

At the next appointment, Allison had lost more weight and was down to ninety-one pounds. The therapist looked at Allison and said, "Sorry, kiddo. You didn't do what you had to. I'm admitting you to the hospital. Your body mass index, BMI, is getting dangerously low."

Allison felt like crying. But even that she could no longer do. Her emotions were numb. Her tears had dried up along with her laughter. So she just sat there listlessly. Her parents looked at her. To Allison, their looks said, "What is *wrong* with you?"

Allison stayed in the hospital for three weeks. She had to get her weight up to one hundred pounds before they would release her. The doctors threatened that they'd insert a feeding tube if she didn't eat. This threat, combined with a better therapist, helped her start eating solids regularly for the first time since she had gotten her wisdom teeth out. Finally, she hit one hundred pounds. She left the hospital.

Her parents found a new therapist. Allison did okay for the next month. She even went to school for a week or so. But then one night, she got on the scale and saw that she weighed 104 pounds. She almost had a panic attack right then and there. She was gaining all the weight back! She knew it. She had to go back on the liquid diet. This time she was smarter about it. She took food on her plate during meals and came up with ingenious plans of getting rid of it, like slipping it up her sleeves and then dumping it down the toilet. Her parents were so happy that she seemed to be doing better, they let their vigilance down.

At the next therapy appointment, Allison's weight was down

to ninety-eight. She claimed that she was wearing lighter clothes that day. The therapist said that from now on, they would have to weigh her in her underwear. Allison felt degraded and vowed to maintain her control the only way she knew how — by not eating.

Everything began to deteriorate again. This time, Allison's weight dropped to eighty-eight pounds. She was admitted to the hospital again, where her weight dropped even further. She now weighed eighty-five pounds and looked horrific. Her bones were protruding all over her body. Everything looked sharp — sharp elbows, sharp hip bones, sharp cheekbones — all poking out of pinched skin. But the worst were her eyes. If you looked in them, you could get lost. Lost in a vast, stormy sea that was eerily silent.

Allison was in her own world. She did not participate in therapy. Not in group therapy. Not in individual therapy. And not in family therapy. She just sat there in stony silence. The only way that any doctors or nurses could make headway was by threatening to insert a feeding tube.

"You can't do that against my will!" Allison said.

"I am sorry, but we can," the nurse responded calmly.

"Well, I'll just rip it out!"

"Then we will have to tie your hands down. Look, Allison, we are doing this for you — we don't want you to die."

Allison felt like she was going to explode. But it worked. She ate to avoid the feeding tube. Again, she slowly gained back weight. This time it took two months until she reached one hundred pounds. The doctors released her, but told her mother that unless she could find an inpatient treatment center that could help her, Allison's life was at significant risk. One of the doctors gave her a pamphlet about Rainbow Eating Disorder Clinic in New Jersey. She said that she'd had another patient who had been in a very bad state whom she had sent there. This patient had recovered.

Allison's mother waited until Allison's weight dropped to under ninety pounds again. Then she called.

≈

Lori put down the folder. Allison sounded like an enigma. What had triggered the anorexia? She had not been seen by very good therapists, and at this point she was severely anorexic. But Rainbow Clinic had helped patients who had been in worse states than Allison. Lori was confident that they could help her.

CHAPTER 3

"Hi, Lori. How were your past couple of days?" Dr. Wilson was sitting back in his chair, arms resting on the armrests, as Lori entered the office.

"Okay." Lori again felt somewhat awkward. She sat down shifting her gaze around the room, not feeling sure where to rest her eyes. Her original feelings of inadequacy returned, making her question being there. Somehow, the tone of Dr. Wilson's question felt condescending. She tried to swallow her pride.

"Well?" he looked at her. He was allowing Lori to steer the session, waiting for her to give it direction.

Lori was now staring out the window behind Dr. Wilson. The sun was beginning to set, and the sky was a striking array of pinks and purples. It almost matched the lilac ruffled blouse that Lori was wearing.

She moved back in her seat, and finally looked toward Dr. Wilson again. "I'd like to start where we left off last — continuing with some early memories. I want to help you completely understand my relationship with Hannah." Lori paused. "And my parents."

"So what's next?"

Lori needed no further prompting to continue with her tale.

Hannah was a highly unusual child. It was apparent from the time she was an infant. To Elaine, that is. Sam was more skeptical.

21

"Look, Elaine, we wanted a child for a while. We finally had Hannah. You are her mother, so of course everything she does amazes you," Sam would say.

"No, Sam. She's different. I'm sure." Elaine could not be dissuaded. Hannah just seemed so alert, so aware from the moment she was born. Her brows were always knitted, making her appear like she was concentrating on some deep thought. When there was a conversation going on around her, she would turn her head back and forth, looking at whomever was currently speaking. It looked as though she understood everything. Hannah reached all the developmental milestones early. She said her first word at seven months, although the pediatrician told Elaine she must be imagining it. She walked at ten months, at which point her language exploded. She began using complex sentences and talking about abstract concepts at about fifteen months.

Sam was a math professor at a state college, Elaine a chemistry professor at the same place. Sam came from a family of college professors. No one big, no Ivy League schools, but four generations of professors all the same. Elaine's father was a doctor; her mother was a novelist. Her grandparents were hardworking, blue-collared immigrants. There were various stories of genius on both sides of the family: an uncle here, a cousin there. Giftedness was definitely in the genes. So it was not a long jump to assume Hannah may have gotten some of those genes. Sam just thought Elaine was reading into things way too early.

But when Hannah taught herself to read at only two and a half years, it became apparent to everyone that she was different. She was definitely "gifted" in some way. Sam was finally convinced.

One day, Sam sat with Hannah and began to teach her math problems. Amazingly, she caught on with no difficulty. At three and a half, Hannah could add two three-digit numerals in her head. Some relatives were calling her a prodigy. She was already comprehending concepts way beyond elementary school. Everyone had different advice for Elaine and Sam: Skip her into kindergarten for next year. No, skip her into first grade. Find a special school for her. Homeschool her.

Elaine considered each option seriously. Sam was willing to trust Elaine with the decision. However, he just wanted to make sure that Hannah would have a normal social life, and no one would ignore that aspect of her development. Socially, Hannah also seemed different from other kids her age. She was extremely shy and did not seem to have friends. She had an easier time interacting with adults, but did not really know how to communicate with other kids. She could play for hours alone, making up complicated imaginary games. But when she was with other kids her age, it was as if she just shut down and turned off. Elaine felt that Hannah's shyness was a stage, and that when she went to school and was around kids more, things would change.

Elaine found a small private school not too far from where they lived. She called the principal and explained the situation to him. Elaine wanted to know if they would take Hannah into school the following year, although she would be only four. The principal said he'd consider it, but Hannah would need a complete psychological-educational evaluation before he would make a decision.

Elaine scheduled an appointment with a child psychologist. The testing took a couple of sessions. Hannah actually enjoyed it. When the testing was complete, the psychologist wrote up a report and scheduled a meeting with Elaine and Sam to review the results.

The meeting was enlightening to both Elaine and Sam.

"Your daughter's IQ, based on the Stanford-Binet, is 167, using a hand scoring procedure to determine an Extended IQ. This places her in the genius level. Only one in eleven thousand scores in this range. She enjoys learning independently and prefers complex challenges. I am sure you are aware of her advanced math and reading abilities. She's able to discuss many things that children her age are not even aware of. She is a perfectionist and is keenly observant.

"Hannah is an introvert. However, seventy-five percent of kids with IQs in the genius range are introverted, compared to thirty percent of the general population, so this can be expected. You told me that Hannah has difficulty interacting with kids her age. Her language and thought processes are so much more sophisticated than other kids her age that it'll be complicated for her to play with them. It's not a solution to have her play with older kids, because she isn't socially mature enough. To help her develop socially, you'll have to try to find her peers who are similar on an intellectual level. This is very important to her development.

"My recommendation is to try to get her into Gaddford Academy, a school for highly gifted kids. It's an excellent school where she'll be with peers similar in intellectual levels. There, they help each child progress independently in their learning, and Hannah won't be bored. Tuition is significant, so you'll have to consider this option carefully."

The psychologist put down the report she had been holding

in her hand and leaned forward.

"I wanted to speak to you about one more thing. In the initial interview, both of you brought up some concerns about Hannah's stubbornness and occasional tantrums in which she can't be convinced to change her mind. After seeing the results of this testing, I'm not too concerned about that. Hannah has complex thoughts going on in her head constantly. She isn't deciding anything haphazardly. However, she is only three and cannot always explain or act based on these thought processes.

"It's my feeling that the tantrums are caused by this. Disciplining her is a complicated situation. You can't just say no to her, because her world is so logical and rational. You have to explain things to her, like you would to a teenager. Let's leave this stubbornness issue for now and see if it resolves itself as she grows older."

Elaine and Sam walked out of the meeting with their minds racing. Before the meeting, they'd already known everything the psychologist told them, but only in the back of their minds. Now it was a confirmed fact that their daughter was a genius. After hearing the psychologist talk, it seemed more like a challenge, or even a disability! They had to find the right school, foster the right friendships, use the right discipline techniques... There was a lot to think about.

Two days after this meeting, while they were still processing the new information, Elaine received some startling news. She was pregnant. This was not a planned pregnancy and Elaine felt completely overwhelmed. She had tried for four years before becoming pregnant with Hannah, going to various doctors and trying numerous fertility treatments. Both Elaine and Sam had been elated when they learned that Elaine was pregnant that first time. This time, Elaine felt almost devastated, aside from the fact that this was shocking — since she should not have been able to conceive without the fertility treatment she had needed the first time.

The first few weeks of the pregnancy, Elaine was almost panicked. Some of that was related to hormones, but the rest of the stress was related to everything going on; Elaine just couldn't understand how another child could fit into her life. They had an unusual child who would need lots of attention. It just didn't seem like they could find the time or resources for another.

Elaine considered an abortion, but only for a fleeting nanosecond. She and Sam were both pro-choice, but only because they believed that each woman should be allowed to make a personal decision about such a personal matter. Elaine knew how strongly Sam felt about abortions. And even though she wished she felt differently, in this instance she completely agreed with him. For them, this would be the wrong choice. Although a fetus is not a person, it is a potential person and killing it is a serious matter.

Over the next couple of months, Elaine calmed down somewhat and Sam even began to grow excited about the new baby. However, Elaine swore to herself that she would not allow this new baby to impede or detract from Hannah's development.

After filling out applications, attending a school tour, and bringing Hannah for an interview, Sam and Elaine were notified that Hannah was accepted into Gaddford Academy. Elaine gave birth to Lori the day before Hannah's first day of school, and she managed to convince her doctor to release her nineteen hours after giving birth, so she could be home to send Hannah off on her first day.

A few years passed and Hannah was doing well at Gaddford. She made some friends and didn't seem quite so unusual, since she was around similar peers, which was a good thing. Still, her math abilities continued to astound people.

Elaine and Sam's second daughter, Lori, was the polar opposite of Hannah. She was an outgoing, vivacious child, full of life and energy. She was a natural with people; she seemed to have a knack for connecting with every person she encountered. She did not teach herself to read at age two and had trouble counting to twenty at age three. However, friends and family kept telling Elaine and Sam that Lori seemed unusually bright, too. She was very verbal and articulate and seemed to have an unusual grasp of abstract concepts.

When Lori entered pre-K, Elaine and Sam had to find a school for her. Sam thought that it would be nice to have Lori and Hannah in the same school. When he suggested the idea, Elaine, although taken aback, agreed to the concept. After consulting with Gaddford, they were told that the school did not automatically accept siblings had a strict IQ acceptance policy; the cutoff for IQ was 138. Before being considered at Gaddford, the child had to bring a psych-ed evaluation demonstrating an IQ of at least 138 on one of two standardized IQ tests.

It was worth a try, so Elaine and Sam scheduled Lori for an evaluation. Once again, the meeting with the psychologist was enlightening.

"Your daughter's IQ is 135, which puts her in the very superior range. However, this score can be deceiving. Lori actually obtained a verbal score of 154. Her working memory and processing speed were significantly lower and brought down her overall score. This is common in what can be termed the asynchronous development of some gifted children. The 154 score is a more accurate portrayal of her true intellectual potential. Current research is indicating that working memory and processing speed scores can cause IQ scores to be misrepresented. Lori is a unique child and needs to be in an environment that can foster her unique abilities."

As Elaine and Sam drove home, their minds were working at top speed once again. Lori was sitting in the back seat. They should have been more careful not to discuss the results of the meeting with her listening in, but they were not.

"So what do we do now?" Sam glanced at Elaine and then looked back at the road as he continued driving.

"Well, there's nothing to talk about. She can't get into Gaddford with that score."

"I guess she's pretty smart, too, though it's a different league than Hannah. But we knew that already. It's too bad she just missed the cutoff. Is it worth talking to Gaddford?"

"No, Sam. I talked to them before we had this meeting. They said there are absolutely no exceptions. If she doesn't score 138 or above, they won't take her."

Lori sat and listened. She wasn't sure what was going on. All she knew was that somehow she had disappointed her parents, and that somehow she was not like Hannah.

In the fall, Lori entered Canton School as a kindergarten student.

"So," Dr. Wilson broke in, "I'm beginning to understand why Hannah was such a hard act to follow."

"Exactly. Meet the real me: Lori, neglected sibling of a child prodigy." Her tone was bitter, although she hadn't meant it to sound that way.

"I can hear years of pain in that statement." Dr. Wilson looked at Lori in a new way. He seemed intrigued.

Lori felt a twinge of satisfaction. She liked being intriguing. She pondered her feelings for a brief moment. Then she glanced at her watch and noticed that there was only one minute left until the session was officially over. She looked up to see Dr. Wilson gazing at her. She shrugged. "I guess it's time to stop."

"Well, Lori, I can see that we're only just beginning."

Lori gave a half smile, mumbled a quick thank-you, and walked out into the hallway, closing the door behind her.

CHAPTER 4

"Hi, Lori," Dr. Wilson initiated as Lori entered the office.

"Hello." Lori smiled as she placed her purse down on the couch and sat in the same chair where she always sat, the black leather chair to Dr. Wilson's left.

"Anything new?"

"Not really." Lori was sure that Dr. Wilson realized she was avoiding talking about the present. She appreciated that he didn't push her.

"I've been thinking about you and Hannah a lot."

"Really?" The word escaped Lori's lips before she could stop it. She hoped she hadn't sounded too eager.

"Yes. Just wondering what life was like. I've always had an interest in child prodigies. And now I'm suddenly thinking about siblings of prodigies."

"It wasn't easy. I can tell you that."

"What was the hardest part of being Hannah's sister?"

Lori shook her head and sighed. "There were so many difficult aspects. Even just in practical ways."

"What do you mean by that?"

Lori bit her lip and thought for a moment. "There were many facets of Hannah's personality that made life more difficult for me on an everyday basis. Certain things used to drive me crazy." Lori pondered momentarily and then added, "Actually, the way my mom dealt with them probably drove me even crazier than the things Hannah herself did." Her tone was angrier than she had intended.

"You sound angry."

"Yeah, well, I guess it was a frustrating experience for me."

"Can you give me an example?"

Lori breathed in and looked at Dr. Wilson's diplomas hanging on the wall: *PhD, Stanford University.* Interesting. She refocused her thoughts, turned back to him, and began.

It was a Sunday morning. Lori's father was making pancakes in the kitchen for a special Sunday morning treat.

"Girls, pancakes are ready," Sam called upstairs.

Lori came running down and sat at the table. Hannah was busy with something in her room.

Sam called up again, "Hannah, are you coming?"

"Not now. I'm busy. Besides, I told you I don't like pancakes anymore," she called down.

Sam shrugged, looked at Lori, and said, "Then I guess it's just me and you."

"Dad, can I invite Sarah over today?"

"I'm not getting involved in that. Ask Mom."

"But she's still sleeping," Lori moaned.

"She'll be up soon. How are the pancakes? I didn't even a get a thank-you!"

"They're yummy. Thanks, Daddy!"

Lori was in first grade. Her best friend, Sarah, lived down the block. They were always playing together.

An hour later, Elaine was sitting at the kitchen table drinking a coffee and doing the Sunday paper's crossword puzzle.

"Mom, can I invite Sarah over?" Lori asked impatiently.

"It's 'may I.' I think that'll be fine. But if Hannah wants to play, I want you to include her."

"Mo-om, do I have to?" Lori made a face. "She's so weird and she messes up all our games. Why can't she invite her own friends over? Why does she always have to play with me? A fifth grader should not be playing with a first grader."

"Lori," Elaine said sharply, "she's your sister! She doesn't have so many friends and she likes to play with you. Do not call her weird! If you cannot work it out to let her play, then I'm not letting any friends come over."

"That's not fair! You're always so mean to me."

"Excuse me. Don't let me ever hear you talk like that again! Lori, in one second, I'm going to send you to your room."

"Fine, I'll let Hannah play. But only if she asks." She turned around and rolled her eyes so her mother couldn't see.

Lori was playing in her room when the doorbell rang. She sprang up and ran to open the door.

"Hi, Sarah!"

Sarah came bounding in. Immediately, she and Lori were laughing and giggling.

"Let's go play in your tree house," Sarah said.

They ran out into the backyard. Pretty soon, they were walking in and out of the house, carrying food, towels, and toys.

"Lori and Sarah, everything you take outside, you're responsible for cleaning up. No messes left around like last time," Sam called out.

A few minutes later, Hannah came out of her room. "Where's Lori?" she asked her mother.

"She's out in the back."

Hannah went out the back door. Elaine closed her eyes

and sighed, knowing that this would probably end in a fight.

"What are you playing?" Hannah asked.

Lori peeked out of the tree house. "Pirates."

"Can I play?"

Sarah whispered to Lori, "Does she have to?"

Lori whispered back, "My mom said I have to let her."

"Oh, man," Sarah mumbled.

"No secrets! What can I be?" asked Hannah.

"You can be the pirate's pet monkey," Lori said.

Sarah giggled.

"You're so mean!" Hannah grimaced.

"Fine, you can be a pirate assistant. Me and Sarah are the pirate chiefs. We're hiding treasure, but it's really hard because the British have a spy plane that's in the sky trying to find us, so anytime we go out of our ship we have to stay camouflaged so they won't see us."

"That doesn't make sense. There were no planes in the days of pirates," Hannah said.

"Hannah, you can play, but don't ruin our game!"

"Well, you can't play a pirate game with planes. Once planes were invented, it ruined the pirates' ability to escape. That's what stopped them from being able to continue robbing ships without being caught."

"Well, we don't care!" said Sarah.

"You can't play. Go away! You're exasperating me!" Lori had just learned that word and she liked how it sounded.

"I'm telling!" Hannah ran inside.

Lori knew what was coming next.

"Lori, come inside!" Elaine called.

Lori left Sarah to man the fort and ran inside.

"Lori, I told you that you can only invite a friend over if you include Hannah. She said that you're not letting her play."

"But Mom, she's so weird!"

"That's it; I told you not to call her weird! I'm sending Sarah home."

Lori brought herself back to the present.

"So what happened next?" Dr. Wilson inquired.

"What always happened. My mom sent Sarah home, and I moped and fumed the rest of the day, refusing to interact with Hannah."

"Did it ever work out when you had friends over?"

"Rarely. After a while, I stopped inviting friends and went to their houses instead, although sometimes my mom would ask me to let Hannah come along. It was pretty sad, actually. Hannah had very few friends and always seemed to tag along with me, even though I was four years younger. As a kid, I thought it was so annoying. I thought my friends wouldn't want to play because Hannah would be with me. And I was so embarrassed of her."

"That sounds like a tough social situation."

"I always had a lot of friends, though, so I guess I overcame that hindrance. Or persisted despite it. Or persisted because of it!"

"Well, Lori, our time is up for today. Have a good week."

"Thank you." Lori knew that she had done this often herself, but it sure felt strange to have Dr. Wilson end the session so abruptly just because time was up. Lori felt her face flush slightly. She hoped that he didn't notice. Maybe she was embarrassed to be brought back to reality and remember that all she was, after all, a client. Nothing more and nothing less.

As she walked out to her car, her thoughts felt like they were in overdrive. It was hard to get caught up in her past and then have to jump back into the present so quickly. She felt like she had landed a little off after this appointment.

As she entered her car, her cell phone rang. She glanced down. It was David. She was unsure why, but she was not in the mood to speak to him. She answered despite this.

"Hi, David."

"Hi, Lori. How'd your session go?"

Lori became more annoyed. "It was okay. What's up, David? I have to make some work-related calls."

"Okay." Maybe she was imagining it, but David sounded hurt. "Your mom just called. She needs to work out dates for the tickets."

Lori couldn't help it. Her words exploded out of her before she could catch them. "Leave me alone! I'm not ready to commit to going. How many times do I have to tell you that?" She was talking to David like he was a kid and she knew he hated that.

"You know what, Lori? You work with this out with your mom. I'm not getting involved anymore. And furthermore, why don't you talk to your therapist about working on your built-up, misplaced anger against your husband? You sure need help!" *Slam.*

David was gone. He had hung up. Lori felt horrible inside. Why was David always so adept at understanding her emotions? She was the psychologist! It killed her when he did that. She hated him and loved him. He drove her crazy and she admired him more than anyone. Oh, why were human emotions so complicated?

CHAPTER 5

LORI ENTERED THE OFFICE BUILDING and nodded to the security guard at the front desk. She dumped her Starbucks coffee cup into the trash can, then turned and walked over to the elevator. As she pushed the button for the eighth floor, she realized that she was beginning to enjoy these sessions. She was proud to say that she was overcoming some of those initial feelings of embarrassment — admitting that she was a psychologist who needed her own help.

Dr. Wilson, or Ron (she could not decide if she was comfortable calling him Ron when she was using him as her therapist — calling him doctor took away some of the embarrassment) was letting her just talk. While talking, she felt like she was organizing her life — picking out the most significant memories and stacking them up neatly. It felt good to be able to talk about all of them. Was it impacting her on an everyday basis? Not yet, or if it was, barely. But she was sure she'd get there. As she had told her own patients many times over, this was the first step.

"Good morning." Dr. Wilson looked like he had something on his mind. Sure enough, he looked at Lori and said, "I hope you don't mind that I'm bringing this up, but I read in this morning's paper that a book you wrote is coming out today. Congratulations! What's the title?"

"Oh, thank you. It's called *Life as a Shadow: Overcoming*

Anorexia from the Eyes of Three Survivors. It took me many years to put it together. I'm excited about its release." Inside, Lori shuddered. Why did Dr. Wilson have to do this? She was finally feeling less self-conscious, overcoming the strangeness of being an accomplished psychologist reversing her everyday role, when he started the session by reminding her of this awkwardness. She appreciated his tone of awe when he spoke of her work, yet, in this setting, his admiration made her feel uncomfortable that she needed his help.

"Well, I'm looking forward to reading it. If it's anything like your other books, I know I'll truly enjoy it."

"The style is different. But I think you'll still like it." Lori cleared her throat. Dr. Wilson probably thought he was being nice. Or maybe he truly admired her work and wanted to talk about it. Probably it was a mixture of the two. Whichever it was, Lori would have to ignore it.

"I have these two horrible memories from when I was nine years old," Lori blurted out.

Dr. Wilson turned to look at her. "Really?"

"I never shared them with anyone, and I just want to unburden myself." Lori's voice faded, and then without warning she felt a lump forming in her throat. She swallowed hard, desperately hoping not to cry. Not here and not now. She was a strong woman.

Suddenly, she didn't want to share her memory. Dr. Wilson admired her, thought she was great, read her books. And now he was going to know that it was all a facade. That she was really a nobody. She wanted to take back her words. But there was Dr. Wilson, sitting and staring at her. Waiting expectantly.

Lori forced herself to begin talking.

Her mother was away for the weekend at a conference. Lori's grandmother, Linda, had come over on Saturday to watch the girls, because Lori's father was out taking care of some errands and going to a meeting. The girls could technically stay home alone, but their bickering was so constant that Elaine hated the idea of leaving them without supervision.

It was three o'clock in the afternoon. Lori had watched lots of TV, had drawn a few portraits of different animals, and had read a book. Hannah was in her room, practicing math problems for some big math competition. Lori was bored.

"Grandma, can I play dress-up with my mom's clothes?" Lori asked as innocently as possible. She loved looking through her mom's old clothes and trying on weird combinations, pretending she was all sorts of things: a homeless woman, an alien, a fashion model, a teacher, a witch… Lori's mom usually said no, but her grandmother probably didn't know that.

Sure enough, her grandmother said, "Okay. Just put everything back when you're finished."

Lori loved her grandmother. The two had a special bond from the time Lori was little. Linda loved creativity and connected with Lori's free spirit. Linda herself was gifted and creative. She had written several novels, two of which were published. Often, she would pick Lori up and take her on an outing — to a museum, to a park, or to the zoo. She would often chastise Elaine, reminding her that Lori needed attention, too. It was probably Linda who saved Lori's life. Saved her life by believing in her and appreciating her.

Excitedly, Lori went into her parents' bedroom. She pulled out a long black skirt. Today she would be a gypsy. She found a beaded necklace in a drawer. She needed only a scarf, and then her outfit would be complete. She began to rummage through her mother's dresser. She couldn't find a scarf. She wasn't able to reach the top drawers, so she pulled a chair over to the dresser. When she opened the top right drawer, she was surprised to see a neat pile of notebooks. Each one had a number.

Lori took one out. She opened it and turned to the first page. "Today I went for an interview…" it began. Lori put the pieces together and realized it was a diary. Her mother kept a diary. This was interesting. Lori began to read. Her face was blushing as she realized she was invading her mother's privacy. But she couldn't stop herself. Most of it was pretty boring stuff, related to her mother's work. But some of it was interesting, like the entry Lori read about an argument her mom got into with Grandma. Or the entry about an argument with Dad. Or the entry about the night her parents got engaged. Now Lori was really blushing.

But then Lori found an entry that would truly change her life. She had been reading entries from before she and Hannah were born, but she wanted to find a more current one. So she reached down in the stack and pulled one out. She found a lot of entries about how incredible Hannah was as a baby, and how proud and amazed her parents were when she taught herself to read.

Lori wondered what her parents thought about her when she was younger. She reached even farther down and pulled out another book and flipped through it. It was also from before she was born. But wait — she found something. Lori's eyes opened wide. She read, "Today, I found out that I am pregnant. I'm devastated. This was not supposed to happen! I know I will never get an abortion, but I have to admit that this option sounds so appealing. How did this happen? We just can't have another kid. Hannah is special. She needs so much. Another kid! We can't do it. I swear that this new kid will never take away any of my attention from Hannah's needs or development."

Lori's head was whirling. Her mother must have been pregnant with her. She didn't want to have her. Even more, her mom was "devastated" to learn she was pregnant with her. Lori maintained her composure long enough to put all the notebooks back in the drawer as neatly as possible. No one could ever know that she had found them and read through them.

She put the chair back where she found it, took off the long skirt and beaded necklace, and ran to her bed. She pulled her covers over her head and began sobbing. *My mom hates me*, she said to herself. *I always knew it. She loves Hannah and she hates me. She hates me. She hates me!* Her thoughts wouldn't stop.

Hannah heard Lori crying from her room next door. She peeked in and in a rare moment of empathy, asked, "Lori, are you okay?"

At that moment, Lori hated Hannah and wanted her as far away as possible. She hated her so much, she just couldn't answer.

"Grandma, Lori needs help!" Hannah called.

Linda came upstairs and sat on Lori's bed, while Hannah went back to her room. "Lori, what's wrong?"

Lori could never tell her grandmother what she had just read. Her grandmother, whom thought she was great, who loved her. But she had to tell Grandma something.

"I'm scared…that you may die one day," Lori said between sobs.

"Oh, Lori." Linda opened her arms wide and Lori crawled in. "Everyone dies eventually. That's part of life. You're born, you die. But all these special memories we share together — they'll be with you forever. No one can take away those times we had together and you can always go back to them. In that way, I'll always be with you."

Lori rested her head on her grandmother's lap and cried and cried, until she was all out of tears.

"What a memory." Dr. Wilson looked at Lori.

Lori blew her nose and sniffled, but she remained composed. Sharing the memory hadn't been as hard as she had thought. She felt a sense of relief, like when a splinter is extracted from deep in the skin.

"My relationship with my mom was never the same after that. There was this unspoken wall between us, this barrier. Sometimes I wonder what would have been if I hadn't read that entry… I think maybe my mom would have gotten past those initial feelings. But after I knew it, I could never let her. So that's how I lived. To my mom, Hannah was always the priority; I was always second. In some strange way, I accepted it.

"Oddly enough, sometimes my relationship with my dad felt even more painful. I felt like he cared about me and loved me, and Hannah did not take away from that. However, Hannah and my dad shared a bond that I could never compete with. My dad had a love of math — he was a math professor! He would constantly challenge Hannah with math problems and would derive great pleasure from her amazing ability, since she was very little, to find answers to the most difficult questions. He would share insights with her. I could never break into this bond. I'd feel like an outsider, and felt so jealous knowing I could never share my dad's greatest enjoyment with him like Hannah could. It was almost worse than my mom's lack of love for me. Because I knew he loved me, but I couldn't get it."

"Did you ever talk to your mom about the diary entry? I mean, did you ever have the courage to confront her?" Dr. Wilson seemed genuinely interested.

"No. I wanted to. I practiced and practiced so many different ways to say it."

"Do you think you ever will?"

"I hope so."

CHAPTER 6

LORI CLOSED THE DOOR TO the office.

"Hi, Lori," Dr. Wilson said as he looked up and smiled.

Lori sat down and smiled back.

"How have you been?"

"Good," Lori stated. Her tone implied nothing.

Dr. Wilson waited and then said, "Well, if you have nothing in the present that you want to discuss, then I'm anxiously awaiting the second memory."

"That sounds good to me." Lori felt her self-esteem plummet. Dr. Wilson had not mentioned her book. Hadn't he said he would read it by today and comment on it? Did that mean that he read it and didn't like it? Or worse, did seeing the human side to Lori make Dr. Wilson lose his professional respect for her?

What was Lori's problem? First she was upset when he mentioned the book, and now she was upset when he didn't. Besides, the book had gotten positive reviews and was selling well. It didn't matter if Dr. Wilson liked it or not. She had to have greater self-worth than that! But it gnawed at her that he didn't comment.

She swallowed hard and began her next memory.

Lori sat with her feet dangling over the edge of the pool.

"Team, listen up! This is important stuff." Coach Ashley looked at the kids in front of him. "We have two weeks until

43

our biggest meet of the year. The best swimmers from the state will be competing in all different categories. We have a lot of potential winners in our group. We need to focus!"

Lori moved her leg slightly, but enough to splash some water on Isaiah, the boy sitting next to her. She giggled. They had an ongoing game — to see who could splash the other last without getting caught by the coach.

"We're going to do an extra half hour of practice every day from now until the Sunday of the meet. Remember to tell all your relatives to come. The more people we have cheering for our team, the better. Okay. Everyone in the water. I want to see thirty laps: five crawl, five breast, five back, five butterfly, ten of anything."

Lori loved swim team. It was a great outlet for her. She took a bus straight from school to the swim club every day of the week. She started doing this when she was six, when her parents had to find somewhere for her to go after school. Hannah finished school later and this way, their mom could pick them up together straight from work.

At first, Lori just signed up for the free-swim program. She was allowed to swim and do homework at the facilities until her parents came. Twice a week, she took swim lessons. But the swim teachers thought she was really good, so after she'd learned all the strokes, she joined the swim club's swim team. They had practice every day and were known for producing really good swimmers. Now, at age nine, Lori was a pro. She often came in first or second for her age group. This swim meet that was coming up was different, though. All the best swimmers from the state would be participating.

Lori dove into the water and began her laps. After a tiring day of practice, she climbed out of the pool. Shivering, she hurried to get her towel. She was about to head into the locker room, when Coach Ashley tapped her on the shoulder.

"Good work today, Lori. Just want you to know: If you swim your best on Sunday, you have a great chance of winning the four-hundred-meter front crawl." She gave Lori a pat on the back and added, "I haven't seen your parents in a while. Tell them I'm looking forward to seeing them."

Although she was still shivering, Lori felt warm all over. She ran to get dressed, feeling almost giddy. Swimming took her into another world. A place where she could hide from the rest of her life. She loved the silence under water. She would dive deep and relish the absolute stillness of the underwater world. Lori was lucky. Not only did she enjoy swimming, she was good at it, too. A natural.

Lori got dressed, grabbed her bag and backpack, and ran outside to wait for her mother. She sat on a bench in front of the swim club building next to Isaiah, who was waiting for his mom.

"Do you think any of us will really win?" Isaiah asked Lori.

Lori shrugged. "You could win the back crawl. Don't you think?"

"Did you ever think about swimming in the Olympics?"

"Nah. There's no way I could."

"Why not? My dad said if I win at least one race at this meet, he'll get me a private coach."

Just then, Lori's mom pulled up. "See you tomorrow," Lori called and jumped into the car. Then she threw her bags onto the floor.

"Careful! You hit my leg!" Hannah called out.

"Sorry!" Lori said in a mocking tone.

"Girls! You have to start arguing already? Lori, how was your day?" Elaine sounded tired.

"Okay." Lori couldn't decide if she should bring up the meet right now. She really wanted her parents to come, but she had to ask at the right time. She ended up blurting out, "We have a big swim meet in two weeks. Can you come?" She just couldn't hold it in.

"Sure, I would love to."

That was easier than she thought. Lori's parents hardly ever came to her meets. There was always something going on. Lori got the feeling that they didn't think swimming was that great. Or they didn't think she was a great swimmer. But this time, her mother agreed right then and there!

After dinner that night, Lori was playing in her room when her mom walked by.

"Oh, Lori, give me the date for your swim meet so I can put it in my calendar."

"It's not this Sunday, but the next one."

"Uh-oh. That's a problem."

Lori's heart sank. She should have known it would not be that simple.

"Hannah's math competition is that Sunday. You know, the one she's been practicing for all these months."

Lori felt disappointed. But more than that, she felt mad. Hannah always stole her parents from her. "It's not fair!! You always go to all of Hannah's things and you never come to mine!" She slammed the book she was holding onto the floor.

"Lori," Elaine said sharply, "first of all, speak respectfully! Second of all, I try my best to come to anything you ever ask me to come to. I'm really sorry, but this is a huge math competition.

Hannah is getting a world ranking in math. Last year, she came in eighty-seventh in the world. She has the chance to move up significantly this year and she needs our support."

"Well, you go to hers and Dad can come to mine."

"Lori, honey, I'm really sorry, but it's not going to work out. Dad needs to be there, too. This is a very big deal. We'll find another swim meet that we can come to," she finished as her tone mellowed slightly.

Lori bit her lip so she wouldn't cry. It was just not fair! She should have known they wouldn't come. Why had she even asked her mother in the first place?

At dinner two nights later, Elaine brought up the swim meet again. "Lori, I was thinking about your swim meet. Maybe Grandma would take you. Wouldn't that be nice?"

Lori knew her mom must be feeling guilty. She shrugged. She didn't want to give her the satisfaction that another idea could make her happy. But secretly, she brightened up inside.

As soon as dinner was over, Lori called her grandmother. "Hi, Grandma."

"Hi, dear. Is this Lori?"

"Yeah."

"How are you?"

"Good. I have a big swim meet coming up, and my mom and dad have to go with Hannah to a math competition, and we're supposed to bring family to cheer for us, so can you come with me?"

"Oh, I would love that, Lori. We can have a day out together! When is it?"

"Not this Sunday, but next Sunday."

"I wish I could come with you, but I'm going out of town

that weekend. I'm going to visit Aunt Lisa. I'm really sorry."

"That's okay. Well, I have to go now."

"Bye, honey. I love you."

Lori hung up the phone. Her heart sank again. She'd be the only kid at the meet with no family to cheer her on. Maybe she should just skip it altogether.

That night, Lori had a dream that she was swimming in the Olympics. When the race was about to begin, she glanced into the crowd and realized her parents weren't there. She didn't know anyone in the audience. Everyone was staring down at her with angry faces. She got up and ran out of the pool.

Friday before the meet, Elaine was driving Lori and Hannah home from swimming and school. "Lori, I made arrangements for Sarah's mom to bring you to the meet. Sarah's going to come, too. They're excited to watch you race. Now you'll have people to cheer for you, after all. Wasn't that a great idea?"

"Oh," Lori mumbled and continued staring out the window.

"Don't I get a thank-you?"

"Thank you, Mom," Lori said, almost sarcastically.

It was finally Sunday. Lori was sitting with her group, waiting for the four-hundred-meter front crawl. She'd already swum the two-hundred-meter front crawl and had placed eighth. Coach said that was great. But the next race was the one in which she had the greatest chance of placing first.

Everybody lined up at the stands at the edge of the pool. Lori tried to review her perfect stroke in her mind. She did better at the four-hundred-meter because she had a lot of stamina. The starting bell rang and the racers were off. Lori pushed herself as hard as she could. It looked like the swimmer to her right was ahead of her, but Lori did not slow down. As she was completing the fourth lap, she gave it everything she had, pulled ahead at the last second, and grabbed the wall just ahead of the swimmer on her right. Had she won?

She lifted her goggles off her eyes and looked up at the scoreboard. It was fun to compete in these fancy races with an electric scoreboard. Third place? Lori felt a lump form in her throat. She'd wanted to win so badly. She'd wanted to come home and tell her family, "I placed first!" She needed them to know she was really serious about this swimming thing.

Who had placed first? She looked around. The two girls at the end of the pool had placed first and second. They were a lot bigger than Lori.

Dejectedly, Lori climbed out of the pool. She was not in any more races that day. She headed to the locker room to change. As she was walking, a man stopped her.

"Hey, I watched you swim. You were great!"

Lori just shrugged.

"Don't be so hard on yourself! This was your first year in this state meet. You can't expect to win right away." The man looked at her with interest. "I'd like to talk to your parents. Where are they sitting?"

"They're not here."

"Not here? So who brought you?"

"My friend's mother."

"Listen, I watched you swim, and I think you have great potential. I'd love to coach you. Here's my card. Please give it to your mom or dad and tell them it's very important to call me."

"But I didn't win." Lori was confused.

"Look, I told you I watched you swim, and I know talent. Your stroke needs a little fine-tuning. That's all. Every year, a few of the kids I coach make it to the nationals. I've had kids I coach swim in the Olympics. Trust me — you have potential."

Lori looked up in wonder. Olympics? She had potential for the Olympics? Then she remembered. There was no way her parents would go for this. She took the card and walked into the locker room. As she was changing, she got mad at her parents again. Why hadn't at least one of them come with her?

A short while later, Sarah's mom pulled into Lori's driveway. "Bye, Lori! You did great! We'll see you later."

"Thanks for taking me, Mrs. Willis. Bye, Sarah!"

"Bye, Lori!"

Lori slammed the car door and ran up to her house, her swim bag bumping into her knees. Her mom opened the door and waved.

"Lori! How was it?"

"Okay." Lori avoided her mom's gaze.

"How did you do?"

"Fine. I came in eighth, fifth, and third in three different races."

"That's great!"

"What happened to Hannah?"

"We won't know how Hannah placed for a few weeks."

A few days later, Lori and her mom were sitting at the table eating a snack before dinner.

"Mom," Lori started hesitantly, "let's say I was a really good swimmer. Would you get me a coach and training so I could go to the Olympics?"

"Lori, do you know how hard it is to make it to the Olympics? Do you know how many kids think they'll end up there and never get close? How much time, effort, and money it takes to try to pursue that dream that's almost as impossible as winning the lottery?"

"So you're saying you wouldn't help me?"

"Honey, do you know how many hours a week you'd have to practice swimming? We'd have to drive you, pick you up, take you to meets, hire coaches... I don't even know what! It's just not realistic in our lives."

"Why? Because you give up your whole lives helping Hannah on a one-in-a-million chance that she'll become some math wizard who invents a new math theory? Well, I deserve to go for a one-in-a-million chance, too!" Lori ran to her room, crying. She found the coach's card that she was supposed to give to her parents. She crumpled it into a ball and threw it in her trash can.

At swim club the next day, Lori was sitting next to Isaiah.

"Lori, guess what! My dad signed me up with this coach who trains kids who go to the nationals every year. I'm starting next week!"

"So? Do you know how hard it is to make it to the Olympics? It's basically impossible. And you'll have to train tons of hours a day."

"Well, one day I'll be swimming in the Olympics. Watch out!"

Lori finished her story.

Dr. Wilson looked at her. "So what happened? Did you continue swimming?"

"Just what I'd always been doing. Swimming on that swim team, my parents rarely showing up at meets, winning some meets here and there. After a while it got old. I still swim, but just for exercise or as an outlet."

"And what happened to Hannah? Where did she place in the math competition?"

"You see that? After all I told you, you're interested in Hannah's math! Just like everyone always was."

Dr. Wilson gave Lori a look.

"Just joking. Anyway, Hannah placed twenty-seventh in the world. It was pretty exciting. Especially since the contest was for ages twelve through eighteen, and Hannah was thirteen."

"I don't think you were joking."

"Yeah, I know. Sometimes I get irrational like that."

"And what happened to Isaiah?"

"He swam in the nationals four years in a row. He never made it to the Olympics, but one year he swam in the world championships. Then he went to college on a swimming scholarship. After that, I lost contact with him."

"Well, Lori, this is thought-provoking. So your anger in this memory is once again directed at your parents."

"Yes," Lori said sadly.

"What made you the angriest?"

"Isn't it obvious? That my parents always put Hannah's dreams and aspirations before mine. That her needs were always first and mine were always second. That I was always inferior in my parents' eyes." This time, the tears came pouring out. Lori couldn't keep them in any longer.

Dr. Wilson sat quietly as Lori covered her face and cried softly for a couple of minutes. Finally, she took a deep breath and looked up.

Dr. Wilson spoke in a very quiet voice. "That sounds so painful, Lori."

Lori nodded and looked down at the floor. She wished she

didn't care. She wished she was so strong that her parents' lack of love had no impact whatsoever. But she was a human and she could not escape her humanity. The years of aching for her parents' adulation were boiling inside her. She picked up another tissue and blew her nose.

"Lori, that was brave of you to relate that. It takes courage to articulate and admit those feelings." Dr. Wilson looked down at his watch, and Lori knew what that meant.

"I'm trying," said Lori as she reached for her purse.

"I hope that we can continue working on all these feelings and memories. Have a great week. Looking forward to our next session."

"Thanks," Lori said as she slowly stood up.

"Oh, by the way, the book was great. I feel funny talking about it now, but I gained a lot of insights from it. I'd love to discuss it with you further in a professional forum, if you wouldn't mind. I have some questions, and I think it can help me as a therapist."

Lori felt relieved. He had read it and liked it. Phew. "I'd be happy to. Just give me a call at my office."

CHAPTER 7

Three Months Earlier

ALLISON LOOKED AROUND THE ROOM. It was orange. All orange. An orange striped blanket. An orange polka-dotted pillow. Orange striped walls. An orange shaggy oval rug next to the bed. An orange metal desk and chair. It was cool. She liked it.

Allison knew that there were red, yellow, green, and purple rooms, too. But there were no blue rooms. One of the other patients had told her that when she'd met her in the dining room a few hours earlier. No one was sure why. Maybe they couldn't get blue furniture. Or maybe blue symbolized sadness. Whatever the case, Rainbow Clinic's colored rooms were fun to look at, with or without the blue rooms.

Allison looked at her suitcase. She had no strength to unpack. She rummaged through it, looking for her iPod. She found it, turned on her favorite music, and sat down in bed with her blanket wrapped around her. She was freezing, as always. It didn't matter that it was the middle of the summer. She pulled the rubber band out of her thin blond ponytail and let her straggly hair fall loosely over her shoulders.

So here she was. About to try some new treatment. Treatment. Like she had a horrible disease. The crazy thing was, all she had to do was eat normally and she'd be better. How could that be a disease? Allison's mind swirled. She closed her eyes. Rainbow colors made splashes on her brain waves. Who was she? How did she become this... this...invalid? This girl who was sick — sick in her head? Could they help her here? Did she want help? Allison felt confused and guilty. Her biggest problem was that she wasn't sure if she wanted help. So how could anyone help her, then?

She thought back to her meeting with Melissa couple of hours earlier. Melissa had been assigned as Allison's case manager and main therapist. A small smile crossed her face. No one had ever talked to her the way Melissa had. Treating her like a thinking human being. Almost like an adult. Explaining to her that they understood how this disease ravaged her body and her soul. How it wrapped its twisted fingers around her brain and warped her thoughts. And how a team of therapists would help Allison gain control of her life again. They would help her by letting her lead, by helping her be in charge again. No one would control her — no doctors, no therapists, no parents, and, most importantly, no anorexia.

Allison had never thought about it that way. It sounded good. She felt a glimmer of hope, for the first time in eleven months.

But there was a problem with all this talk. Was the anorexia really controlling her? Sometimes, she thought that anorexia was her only friend in the world. It was the only one who understood her. Allison felt like anorexia was her partner — not the enemy that had to be conquered. She could not imagine living without it.

Her head was hurting. Could she control anorexia, or was it truly a disease? Was anorexia her friend or her enemy? Her eyes were still closed. Suddenly, horrible monster faces started marching around her brain. They were mean, angry creatures, all growling and frowning at her. She opened her eyes as fast as she could. The monsters disappeared. Every once in a while, the monsters came and frightened her. They never talked, so she never knew who they were. Were they symbols of the anorexia, or were they symbols of her family and friends?

Allison needed to sleep. She took her pajamas out of her suitcase and pulled them on. She climbed back into bed. She wanted to stop thinking. She closed her eyes and welcomed sleep.

CHAPTER 8

L ORI SLAMMED HER CAR DOOR shut and looked admiringly at the brand-new silver Honda Odyssey that she and her husband had recently purchased. David and Lori had decided it was time to move on to the minivan stage. They had postponed it long enough. Something about being a minivan-driving soccer mom just felt weird. Oh, well. She'd better get used to it. Because that's exactly what she had become.

Lori looked back one more time, pushed the clicker to lock the doors, and hurried into Dr. Wilson's office building.

"Good morning, Lori." Dr. Wilson was sitting, as usual, waiting with a stack of papers nearby.

"Hi." Lori sat down on the same chair she always sat on.

"So let's see. How have you been sleeping? That can often be an indicator of underlying stress levels."

"Actually, now that you mention it, I have had some episodes of insomnia over the past few months. Recently, however, it has decreased, especially on the days that I meet with you. I think talking to you helps me get out some of these thoughts so they aren't replaying themselves constantly when I'm trying to sleep."

"That's good news."

Again, it was uncomfortably silent. Dr. Wilson was waiting for her to direct the session. Lori looked out the window.

Dr. Wilson broke the silence. "Lori, I'm sure you realize that

57

we're focusing a lot on the past. If you want me to help you, we're going to have to start talking about the present. You know how it is. We can't change the past, but we can work on the present to change the future."

"I know, I know. Just give me a little more time. I'm getting there."

"Well, I promised I wouldn't push you and I won't."

"Thanks for keeping your word."

Dr. Wilson smiled. "I like the positive reinforcement. So what's this memory about?"

"Hannah graduated from Gaddford, a kindergarten through eighth-grade school, at thirteen. Since Gaddford lets kids move at their own level, Hannah had basically completed a high school curriculum by the time she finished elementary and was way beyond in math. She had a few different options for the next year: start college, go to high school, or go to high school but skip a few grades.

"My parents decided to put her into twelfth grade at a private high school. Not because she needed it academically; they thought it would be a helpful social experience before she began college. It didn't work out too well, though. Hannah never made friends and was a social misfit. And, as was predicted, it was a wasted year academically.

"Whatever the case, the next year, she got into a great early admissions program in a college only thirty minutes away from our home. They had a special dorm floor, and a mentor for a group of twenty-five kids who were all the same age as Hannah. It was perfect for her. She would dorm during the week and then come home for weekends. Of course, she was majoring in math. She was pretty happy at first. She felt more normal again with her group of genius peers, finding friends who shared common interests. She would bring some of them home for weekends. Most of her friends were as weird as she was."

"And what did this all mean for you?" Dr. Wilson interjected.

"Well, it was great for me, too, at first. Hannah left and I had my parents all to myself. My relationship with my sister improved significantly. We'd even talk on the phone every couple of days. Things seemed to be going well for everyone.

"Then, in the middle of the first year, about two weeks after Hannah had gone back after winter break, she came home. She was extremely tired and couldn't get out of bed. She went to the doctor, who tested her for mono and other such viruses. All the tests came back negative. But she would just stay in bed all day and sleep. The doctor suggested that she see a psychologist, but Hannah refused. My parents kept threatening to make an appointment, but never followed through. After three weeks of this, she started getting out of bed again.

"My parents and Hannah met with the college to figure out how she should finish the semester. They decided that Hannah would take only two of her original four classes, just to make her load a little easier for the time being. She did this and everything went back to normal for the next year and a half.

"Then it was the fall semester of Hannah's sophomore year. I turned twelve in the beginning of September. Since we're Jewish that meant my bat mitzvah..."

Although Lori's actual birthday was in September, Elaine and Sam had planned a bat mitzvah celebration for the end of October. It was easier this way; then Hannah and Lori could get used to the new school year and settle in before this disruption.

With one week to go before the party, everything was mostly set. Lori was so excited. She'd wanted something big for her party, and her parents had acquiesced. She wasn't sure why, but this was going to be a much bigger party than Hannah had received. Her parents had rented tents, popcorn makers, cotton candy machines, and hot pretzel machines. They even hired a DJ. It was not like her parents to make this kind of party, but Lori had begged and begged for something extra special. Elaine had also let Lori pick out the dress she wanted, which she knew her mother didn't especially like. It felt great that her parents were doing all this for her. Everything seemed perfect.

Monday night before the bat mitzvah, which was to take place on Sunday afternoon, Hannah called home. She had stayed in school over the weekend to get some work done. She wasn't feeling well and was thinking that the "tired thing" was coming back. She couldn't get out of bed and wanted to come home.

Elaine called Sam at work. They began arguing over the phone. Elaine thought that Hannah should stay in school and try to stick it out. Sam thought she should come home, and maybe this time she'd go to some sort of therapist. Lori sat on the couch, pretending to read a book, as she listened to her mom's voice rise. Her heart sank. Somehow, Hannah would find a way to ruin her bat mitzvah. She just knew it.

By Tuesday night, Hannah was hysterical on the phone. She couldn't get out of bed. She needed to come home. Even though she'd gotten her license over the summer, she hadn't gotten a car yet. So Sam went to pick her up.

For the rest of the week, Hannah stayed in bed, sometimes hysterical and crying, sometimes sleeping passively. Sometimes she would mumble things about not wanting to live. She barely ate. Sam was very nervous and took off work. He didn't want Hannah to be home alone in this state of mind. Elaine agreed that Hannah needed to see a psychologist, but the psychologist they were referred to was booked until the Wednesday after the bat mitzvah.

Elaine had lots of last-minute details to take care of for the party, but it was really hard with the crisis going on at home. Elaine's mom came to help out and took Lori around to buy all the last-minute things, like shoes. Lori had fun with her grandmother, but there was a dark cloud hanging around their house, casting a shadow over everything. Lori could see the worry creases in her parents' faces growing sharper by the day. It was hard to listen to Hannah like this. She was obviously in tremendous pain, so Lori felt guilty. Guilty because she was feeling particularly angry at Hannah.

Once again, it wasn't fair. Hannah had used up so much of her parents' attention all their lives because of her special genius. And now this? Now she had to steal more attention from Lori? If she kept this up until Saturday, she'd ruin Lori's bat mitzvah. It was *not fair*! Lori was mad, mad, mad.

On Friday, Hannah got out of bed for the first time in days. She put on a bathrobe and came downstairs without crying or screaming. Lori breathed a sigh of relief and crossed her fingers. Maybe, just maybe, Hannah would be better in time for the bat mitzvah. Lots of relatives were coming in for the weekend and staying at a hotel nearby. Hannah had instructed her parents and Lori not to discuss her current state with anyone. If anyone asked, they all agreed to say Hannah had a virus.

Saturday morning, Lori woke up and felt warm all over.

It was the day of her party. She walked over to her closet and looked at her dress and shoes all lined up. This was it. Her special day.

Then she heard Hannah sobbing hysterically. She could hear her all the way in her room.

"I just want to die. I can't take it anymore. No, no, no!!"

Sam was in there, and Lori heard him respond, "Hannah, just pull yourself together. If you take a shower and eat breakfast, you'll feel better. You've got to stop doing this to yourself. Besides, it's not fair to Lori! Just control yourself for today." Sam sounded worried — well, worried, and maybe just a little exasperated.

"I can't, I can't, I can't, I can't!!" Hannah was screaming.

Lori squeezed her eyes shut. Maybe Hannah was doing it on purpose. Maybe she was trying to ruin her bat mitzvah. Lori felt madder than she had ever felt. How could Hannah do this?

And then the guilt came.

A few minutes later, Lori heard her mom walk into the room and say, "Hannah, you have got to pull yourself together. Everyone experiences rough times. We're taking you to the therapist on Wednesday. But until then, just keep it together. You are not a baby!" Elaine sounded worried, too — well, worried, and maybe just a little mad herself.

Hannah wailed louder. She sounded like the whistling wind before a full-blown tornado lands. Then, somehow, she calmed down and fell back asleep.

The day passed. Workers came and set up the tents and all the machines. Lori got dressed. A photographer showed up. The guests began arriving. The bat mitzvah began. In the end, Lori had a great time, although Hannah never came downstairs.

Sam checked on her periodically, and Lori tried her best to block herself from thinking about Hannah. It was awkward answering questions about Hannah's whereabouts, but Lori just told everyone that she'd come down with a really bad virus.

Lori breathed in slowly, clasped her hands together, and looked down. "I have a lovely picture from the bat mitzvah that I used to treasure. It's a picture of me between my parents. Their arms are around me and I have this huge smile on my face. But recently, I haven't been able to look at it. If you look close enough, you can see the worry on my parents' faces. And my smile is a little too big — you can almost tell I'm hiding something. I so badly wanted it to be a perfect day. It just wasn't. I know it wasn't Hannah's fault, but I can't get past it."

"Why do you think it wasn't Hannah's fault?"

"Oh, come on, Dr. Wilson. Are you playing games with me? How could it be her fault? She was in terrible pain. We're psychologists. You know as well as I that depression is a real illness."

Dr. Wilson looked at Lori and knitted his brow. He didn't say anything.

"Okay, you're right. In the recesses of my mind, I feel like she did it on purpose. I know it can't be, but she must have — just at the right moment she managed to get depressed. Just when I finally had my parents' attention." She paused. "I don't think it was a conscious decision, but subconsciously, in some warped way, she made it happen." Lori's voice was shaking.

"So did the psychologist help Hannah?"

"Well, my parents had to drag her to her first appointment. She got there very late because she couldn't get out of bed. It was only when my parents threatened to call an ambulance and have her taken to a mental ward in the hospital that she was able to get up. After her first appointment, the psychologist spoke to Hannah's pediatrician, and she started some sort of medication, probably Zoloft. She went to the psychologist twice a week for a while and slowly got back to herself. She couldn't go back to college for the rest of the semester.

"Once again, my parents and Hannah met with the college. Somehow, in therapy, she realized that she wanted to change majors. She wanted to be involved in a profession through which she could help the world. So she switched her major to physics. She talked about these big dreams of discovering new theories and changing history. I remember my dad coming home that night and talking about it at the dinner table. I could hear the disappointment in his voice when he said, 'So Hannah, no math professorship in your future.' I felt guilty feeling happy, but I couldn't help myself. I'd always imagined that Hannah and my dad would be math professors in the same college and spend their lunch analyzing theories together."

Lori stopped talking again. "I know my time is up." She looked at Dr. Wilson.

Dr. Wilson glanced at his watch. "Yes, you're right. My next client should be here momentarily. I hope the insomnia continues to decrease. See you next week."

CHAPTER 9

ORI HEADED INTO THE OFFICE building, rushing a little so as not to be late. It bothered her when her own clients were late, and she didn't want Dr. Wilson to feel that way toward her. She reached his office two minutes early and almost bumped into another woman who was leaving. She was slightly overweight, attractive, wearing a black sweater set and a black-and-white flowered knee-length skirt. Lori loved trying to guess people's professions just by looking at them. If she had to make a guess about this woman, she'd say...corporate lawyer. The woman mumbled a terse hello, barely noticing Lori. She looked upset. Lori opened the door and saw Dr. Wilson, standing, looking upset, too.

Lori felt awkward. This was the strangest part of the therapeutic relationship — for her, at least. Here she was spilling her guts to this man, telling him her deepest fears, her innermost emotions — and she couldn't even ask him if he was all right. Who knew what was going on in his life? Was Dr. Wilson in the middle of a divorce? Or had he just gotten into a normal argument with his wife? Or maybe this was some other woman completely? The possibilities were endless.

Dr. Wilson tried to smile and readjust himself. He sat down, breathed deeply, and said, "How are you, Lori?"

"Good, good." Lori sat down, too. She felt guilty saying things were good when things may not be good for her therapist. She was trying to act as normal as possible, pretending she hadn't noticed anything unusual.

"You know, I'm really caught up in your story. It's quite interesting and you have a captivating way of telling it."

"Thank you... I guess."

"So here's what I was wondering. How did you become so successful, so academically successful, with all those issues in your background and self-esteem?"

"Good question. It's another story just like everything else. I can actually pinpoint an incident that had a significant impact on me. My life could have turned out the same without it, but somehow I don't think it would have."

Lori was standing in the bathroom with Sarah and another friend, Brianna. They were laughing pretty hard. Some crazy joke only teenage girls could get. It was in the middle of science class. They had all left class on the pretext of having to use the bathroom. Mrs. Venkutachelum was a brilliant, science-loving woman. But she had no clue how to teach a class or control a group of rowdy teenagers. Most days, Lori and some other friends would manage to escape after about fifteen minutes of class. They would meet in the bathroom and stay out for the rest of the period.

Lori was a wild high school junior involved in risky teenage behavior — like smoking weed and drinking. She wasn't failing out of school, but she had about a C average. She rarely did homework or handed in assignments. Frankly, she was lucky she wasn't failing.

She fought with her parents a lot. They didn't like her friends and had suspicions about some of her activities. However, they didn't know how to stop any of it. Her mom would give her speeches about making something with her life; her dad would warn her that she was headed nowhere. But they couldn't get through to her.

So there Lori stood. In the bathroom at two o'clock in the middle of a school day. Brianna pulled out some rolls of weed and handed one to Sarah and one to Lori. Then she pulled out a lighter. They smoked a little. The laughing grew louder and sillier. Sarah tried to shush them. "Lori, Brianna, we better not get too loud. If they catch us, we're dead," she said as she herself laughed some more.

"One second. I gotta go." Lori pointed to a stall and then walked in and closed the door. Just then, the main door to the bathroom creaked open. "Sarah, Brianna, follow me!" Ms. Sturgis, the school counselor, spoke sharply. Lori trembled inadvertently in the bathroom stall, hardly daring to move. Had Ms. Sturgis realized there was someone else in the bathroom? Would Sarah and Brianna give her away? The bathroom door creaked closed. Lori was left alone. She waited another ten minutes and slipped out herself.

She'd only smoked for a brief minute, so she was barely high. She tried to maintain her composure as she wondered what would happen to Sarah and Brianna. The school's rules were pretty clear: If you were caught with drugs in school, you would be expelled. A horrible pang of guilt overwhelmed Lori. How would it be fair if they got kicked out and she got away scot-free? Would her friends ever talk to her again? She almost wished she had been caught, too.

She didn't have to wait too long to find out what happened. She walked over to her locker and saw Sarah and Brianna packing up their stuff. Their tear-streaked faces told the story. "Sarah," Lori called out, "what's going on?"

Sarah looked at Lori. "We're suspended for a week. They don't know it's weed. They think it's regular cigarettes. They're so stupid, aren't they?"

Lori breathed a sigh of relief. "It's weird how I got away with it, you know? So why are you guys crying?"

Brianna looked at Lori. "Well, I started crying because I thought they for sure knew it was weed, and this was the end of my school career here. Besides, my parents would kill me! But when I realized they didn't know, I had to keep it up so they wouldn't guess the truth. Sarah joined in the act." Brianna looked to Sarah and they both controlled a giggle.

But then Sarah grew serious. "My mom and dad are still going to kill me. Darn! Why did we have to get caught?"

The next day, Ms. Sturgis showed up during math class. Everyone looked up as she walked into the room. "I'd like to see Lori Josephson, please," she said and looked at Lori with a grim face. Lori's heart stopped. So she was caught, after all. Who would be madder, her mom or dad? Her mom would yell more, but her dad would be more disappointed. Oh, well. Lori's stomach churned. She stood up and walked to the front of the room. She could feel everyone's eyes on her.

"Follow me, please," Ms. Sturgis said curtly.

Lori walked behind her, trying to keep up with her pace. They reached Ms. Sturgis's office. Ms. Sturgis opened the door and motioned to Lori to walk in ahead of her. Lori sat down on the chair in front of the school counselor's desk. Ms. Sturgis sat down, too. The silence was deafening.

"Lori, I have something to talk to you about."

Lori wished she would just spit it out already. She hated the suspense.

"I'm not sure how to explain this." Ms. Sturgis continued looking at her. "I know you were in the bathroom smoking with Sarah and Brianna. I saw your shoes under the door of the bathroom stall."

Lori began to sputter.

Ms. Sturgis held up her hand. "Wait. Don't say anything. I didn't tell Ms. Holcum or Mr. Westell. I'd like to ignore this little episode. No one on staff knows you were there, and I don't intend to tell them. But I'd like to ask for a favor in return."

Lori looked at Ms. Sturgis with curiosity.

"Yesterday, right before I went searching in the bathroom, I actually came looking for you in your science class. I had something to discuss with you. When I realized you were out, as were Brianna and Sarah, I got suspicious and searched out the bathrooms, knowing I had to stop any trouble, but hoping you wouldn't be doing anything stupid. Luck was behind you that you just missed me. And luck was behind me that I didn't have to get you in trouble.

"I first came to find you because we just got the SAT scores back. I reviewed each student's score. Yours really shocked me." She paused, looking at Lori keenly.

"You got a 780 out of 800 in English! Do you know how high that is? It's the highest English score in your grade. But then I looked at your grades. You have a C average in English. Does that make sense to you?" Ms. Sturgis stared at Lori.

Lori stared back. "You must have seen the wrong scores."

Ms. Sturgis pushed a copy of Lori's scores in front of her. There it was, glaring right at her: 780.

"Ms. Sturgis, you don't get it. I have a sister who is a total genius — like the child prodigy kind. She started college before fifteen, she reads math theories for leisure, and she is majoring in physics. I'm the complete opposite. Don't get me wrong — I have good self-esteem. I know my strengths: I'm pretty, I'm lots of fun to be around, I have lots of friends, I'm a good swimmer. But I am not a genius."

"Lori, it's you who doesn't get it. You are brilliant. You couldn't score that high without being brilliant. So now add 'smartness' to your list of talents."

"Yeah, whatever." Lori looked down. If she remembered correctly, Hannah had scored an 800 in math, but only a 750 in English. Lori remembered those numbers because they'd been a big deal. That meant Lori actually scored higher than Hannah. It didn't make sense.

"So here's my offer. I'll never tell anyone about the bathroom, but you promise me that you'll try your hardest this semester, just in English class. I'd love to make you a bet that you can get an A."

What could Lori do? She had no choice but to agree.

"Well, did you get an A?" Dr. Wilson couldn't resist asking.

"Yes, I actually ended up with a ninety-seven average. I did all my work that semester, handed in all my homework, and studied for all the tests. My grades in all my other classes were still Cs. But this experience proved something to me. My teacher was extremely complimentary about my writing abilities, and I began to think that maybe I could become a novelist like my grandmother. For one of the first times in my life, I felt smart.

"The next year was my senior year. Other than English, my

grades were not the best, but with my SAT score and really good application essays, I got into some decent colleges. My parents were pleased and surprised. I think Hannah was surprised, too."

Lori knew that the session was over without even glancing at the clock. She could tell by the way Dr. Wilson was gathering his papers together.

"Well, Lori, I guess I'll get to hear about your college experiences next session."

Lori reached for her purse and stood up. "See you next week."

CHAPTER 10

Lori opened the door once again. There was Dr. Wilson, ready and waiting. As always.

As she made herself comfortable, Dr. Wilson gave her a smile. "So, as usual, you left me with something to think about. Obviously, you were successful in college because you ended up with a PhD. But how did you manage it? And where was Hannah all that time?"

"The college that I chose was about a three-hour drive from my home. My parents were excited, yet skeptical at the same time. I think they had envisioned me flipping burgers at McDonalds. My mom kept warning me that if I partied and failed out of school, they wouldn't let me move back home. I was unsure of my major, but was leaning toward English, as I was hoping to become a novelist.

"When I informed my grandmother of this idea, she was less encouraging than I'd imagined. She praised my writing talent, but warned me that a career as a novelist was not financially stable. She said that it worked for her, because her husband was a cardiologist and had a reliable salary. But her attitude did not deter me.

"Things started off well. I completely threw myself into my work and was a totally different student than I had been in high school. My first semester, I got all As. I liked my professors and actually enjoyed writing papers. My parents were shocked. Hannah, meanwhile, was having a very difficult time. She'd graduated with a BSc in physics, but it had taken her five years instead of four. She had taken off that one semester in the beginning and then again a couple of years later. She kept experiencing major bouts of depression, in which she would totally shut down. Her grades weren't so good, as she had difficulty concentrating and completing her work. My father kept telling her that she should have majored in math; she would have been happier and done better. But in my opinion, it had nothing to do with that.

"After she graduated, she entered a master's program, again in physics. She'd really been hoping to obtain a doctoral fellowship in some research area in physics. However, with her poor attendance and average grades, she was having trouble finding something in this very competitive field.

"By the time I began my freshman year, Hannah had completed her master's. This time, her grades had improved slightly. She applied again all over, hoping to get a doctoral fellowship. Nothing came through. So during my first semester, when I was doing well academically for the first time in my life, Hannah was at home, falling apart, desperate to continue with what had become her life's passion: atmospheric physics and research involving global warming. Please don't ask me any details about her science career — I have some sort of mental block to understanding science.

"It was really odd when I came home for winter break. I showed my parents my grades — at that point I had a 4.0 GPA — while Hannah seemed miserable, sulking behind us. Suddenly, I was the academic success and Hannah was the failure. I sort of liked the feeling. But it only lasted a few minutes. Then the terrible guilt set in.

"When Hannah wouldn't get out of bed the next day and talked about how she wished she were dead, I just knew it was all my fault. I'd have nightmares about my sister committing suicide and her goodbye note saying, 'I couldn't handle Lori being more successful than me.' But only one week later, Hannah got a job with a college about twenty minutes away. They offered her a position teaching physics. Even though this was a terrible blow to her dreams of academia, she accepted the job. Two weeks later, I left back to school and Hannah began work."

"Wow! Look at that." Dr. Wilson was shaking his head back and forth. "I've always said that child prodigies are rarely successful. I'd love to do a study on how often child prodigies don't develop to their potential."

"Wait! Don't jump to conclusions. This story is far from over."

"I'm just as curious as ever."

"Back in college, I continued to meet success. I declared my major in English. I was doing well, but was isolating myself in a weird sort of way. I had friends, but I totally immersed myself in my studies."

"Did you date any guys?"

"That's a good question." Lori looked up momentarily. "Here and there. I'd see a guy a few times, but nothing ever developed into a real relationship."

"Why do you think you were isolating yourself so much?"

"You know, I think that things at home seemed so chaotic to me that life felt dark and suffocating. I couldn't bring myself to act frivolous — to drink and party like most of my friends. Doing my work was a haven, a way to transport myself into a different world. Also, I gained some weight and didn't feel so good about my looks."

"How did you know what was going on at home?"

"Often when I would call home, I'd hear Hannah screaming in the background." Lori paused as she had a vivid flashback and could almost hear Hannah shrieking right there.

"What do you mean? What was she screaming?"

"Things like 'I can't do this! I don't want to live! I want to give up!' It was strange. I've never heard any other adult act like that. Sometimes she'd just moan and scream words like 'No, no, no!' My parents were consumed with taking care of her. It was like having a baby again, since she needed full-time care. It was so hard to watch, to listen to Hannah act like that and see how tortured and confused my parents were.

"Hannah was able to keep her job, which seemed insane to me. She'd go to class in the evenings and act like everything was normal. If she could control herself when she was teaching, I felt like she must be able to control herself the rest of the day, too. It made me even angrier and more certain that this was some sort of ploy."

"Looking back, what do you think was really going on?" Dr. Wilson's eyes were opened wide like he was trying to figure out a puzzle.

Lori looked dazed. Dr. Wilson had caught her off guard. "I just assumed she was totally crazy. And that it was on purpose."

"I would've thought that with all your training in psychology, you would've analyzed and analyzed her."

"You always think that you can be non-biased and analyze family members when you have the training. But I guess it's still hard."

Lori shook herself, took a sip of water from a water bottle she was carrying, and continued, "At that point, I'd switch from feeling terribly guilty that Hannah was so sick, to being bitterly angry at all the time and energy she was sapping from my parents. It wasn't fair. All her life, she'd found a way to make sure all the energy and time was focused on her. I resented Hannah and I resented my parents. Hannah was an adult. They should have just told her enough is enough, and kicked her out of their house! Or they should've committed her to a psychiatric hospital." Lori's words came out with more anger than she had intended.

"Is that something you would have done as a parent?" Dr. Wilson's soothing voice brought her back to the present.

"I've thought about it many times, and I've come up with many ways that I would have dealt with it differently than they did. But I understand what you're saying. I know I shouldn't judge them. With their resources and limited knowledge, they were certainly doing what they could."

"I didn't say anything about not judging them!"

"But your implications were obvious."

"Back to your story. Did you maintain your high grades?"

"Yes, I actually maintained my 4.0 GPA the next semester, too. I continued to find solace in my schoolwork, while the craziness at home only increased. My dad took off work to stay at home with Hannah and help her out. He had tenure, so the college couldn't fire him, but they took away a lot of his classes. This added to his anxiety and he began to exhibit signs of depression, too. My parents were fighting a lot and my home was in upheaval.

"That summer was awful. I was home from college, working as a swim instructor at a swim club near my house. My school friends were around, but they were all into drinking and partying. I felt different at that point. I just felt lonely and never wanted to join them. Eventually, they stopped calling. I had a few friends who were working at the swim club, and I'd hang out with them. Hannah was having panic attacks, my parents were taking care of her every need — and no one was paying attention to me."

"That sounds like it was an awful time in your life."

Lori breathed deeply. Even after all those years, it felt good to hear someone say that.

"Things began to improve a little, when a miraculous thing happened to Hannah at the end of the summer. She got a phone call from her old physics professor. Apparently, he had gotten a prestigious professorship at MIT and was hiring doctoral students to do research for him. He remembered Hannah's brilliant mind and offered her a position. This was Hannah's dream job. However, at that point she was in such a bad state that she was too nervous to commit. With a lot of coaxing, and help from her therapist, she finally accepted the offer. I left back to school with a new sense of hope for all my family members. But the stresses of the summer would soon take their toll on me."

"Did your grades begin to drop?"

"No. Surprisingly, I maintained my dedication. My issues came out in a different way. I had always been thin and pretty. But during my first year of college, I'd gained about fifteen pounds. I wasn't fat, but I was no longer stick thin. I'm sure you can guess what happened next.

I started a diet that quickly spun out of control. In three weeks, I lost about twenty pounds. In the next couple of months, I stopped getting my period and my hair began falling out. I was getting lots of compliments from friends about how good I looked, and it felt great. I kept cutting back on the amount of calories I would eat a day, until I was down to about eight hundred. I was so careful about not eating one extra calorie that I was scared to lick a stamp! I can vividly recall the feeling of controlling myself from eating even when I was starving. I would get this high — almost like from drugs.

"Then came winter break. I was going home, and Hannah would be there, too."

Lori lifted her suitcase into the back of her red Ford Escort. It seemed so much heavier than last time. Everything seemed to take more effort these days. Oh, well. That was the price she would have to pay for being thin. You can't have everything. Lori went back into her dorm room one last time before she headed out.

"Bye, Sophie! Have a great winter break. Remember to call me. Hope your parents aren't too annoying!"

"Yeah, see you! Enjoy your winter break. Hope Hannah doesn't ruin it for you."

"I think she'll be fine. She seems to be doing better now, and I think she loves her job."

"Take care. Talk to you!"

Lori gave a final look around the room to make sure she didn't leave anything. She lifted her hand in a wave and headed out the door.

The drive home went by pretty quickly. Lori loved the quiet time in the car. She'd always use this time to think and process the semester's events. She had some music playing softly in the background as she contemplated this past semester. She wondered if her parents would notice that she had lost weight. Probably not. They never seemed too interested in her. Especially not with Hannah coming home from her first semester at MIT.

When Lori pulled into the driveway, she saw both her parents' cars. That meant they were back from picking Hannah up from the airport. (They had warned her that one of them may be out when she arrived, because Hannah was arriving at a similar time.)

Lori left her suitcase in the car and headed into the house. Her mom was sitting on the couch and saw her first.

"Lori! Welcome home!" She stood up and gave Lori a big hug. So far so good. The mood in the house seemed happier than it had been in a while.

Then Lori's dad came into the room. "Lori! How was the drive?" He, too, approached Lori and gave her a hug.

"Great! You guys look happy," Lori commented.

"Well, it's great to have our two girls home again. It's been pretty lonely this semester."

Lori could smell dinner cooking. It smelled like...meatballs and spaghetti. Her old favorite. Uh-oh. She hoped her mom wouldn't be too insulted. She wouldn't eat that stuff now.

"Where's Hannah?" Lori asked, looking around.

"She's relaxing in her room. I thought we would have dinner in about twenty minutes. I made your and Hannah's favorite!"

About twenty minutes later, they all sat down at the dinner table.

"So, Lori! How's school treating you? We haven't really spoken in a few weeks. I actually tried to call you a couple of times, but I couldn't get through." Hannah sounded good.

"I know. I've been super busy with end-of-semester papers and finals," Lori lied, sort of. She had been really busy, but that wasn't the only reason she hadn't spoken to Hannah. She was in a pretty antisocial state. Worse than any other semester. Besides, she was annoyed that Hannah could act so normal and pretend that everything was fine when she had ruined their family for a while.

Elaine passed out the food. Lori was in a dilemma. She did not want her mother to get insulted, but there was no way she could eat the meatballs and spaghetti. Way too many calories. She put some on her plate; she didn't want to make a scene.

Everyone started eating.

"It's been so quiet around here! But believe me, we're happy for both of you." Sam was beaming. Lori hadn't seen him this happy in years.

Everyone grew quiet and began to eat. Lori tried cutting the food up into tiny pieces and pushing it around her plate. Could she get away with this?

"Lori, what's wrong with the meatballs? You don't seem to be eating any." Elaine was suddenly looking at her in a scrutinizing way.

"I'm just not too hungry right now."

Her mom gave a quizzical look. "Lori, you actually look very thin. Are you feeling well?"

So she did notice. It had only taken about an hour. "Yeah, I'm fine. Just feeling a little nauseous. May have been the drive. If it's okay with you, I'm going to lie down. Maybe I'll feel better in the morning."

The next few days, Lori spent time catching up on sleep and swimming. It was hard to swim her usual fifty laps, as her energy level was very low. She noticed her mom and dad watching her closely during meals, and giving each other looks every so often.

One night, Lori was lying in bed, reading, when Hannah knocked at her door.

"Can I come in?"

"Mm-hmm," Lori mumbled, not lifting her head from her book.

Hannah slowly opened the door and awkwardly came into the room. Hannah and Lori hardly sat and talked, so this was a little odd.

At first, Lori just ignored Hannah's presence. But after a while, having her there began to get annoying.

"Hannah, uh, what exactly are you doing?" Lori couldn't keep the irritation out of her voice.

"Mind if I sit down?"

"Not at all."

"Where should I sit?"

"On…the chair?" Lori muttered.

Hannah sat down. She looked uncomfortable and unsure of what to say. Lori couldn't help wondering what on earth she wanted.

At long last, Hannah began, "You know, Mom and Dad are really worried about you. You're not eating and you lost a lot of weight. They don't know how to talk to you about it."

Lori felt the fury exploding within her. "So you felt the need to mention it?" Though her voice trembled a little, she kept her tone down.

"Well, I wanted to suggest that you see a therapist. It's not right that you have Mom and Dad so worried."

"Oh, shut up!" Lori exploded. "Who are you to tell me not to worry Mom and Dad? What have you been doing all these years? You, who almost ruined their marriage, their careers, and our family — you are telling me not to worry them?! Get out of my room!" She was screaming and crying at the same time.

Hannah looked shocked. She stood up, started to say something, then changed her mind. She walked out of the room. As she closed the door, she turned around again and then said, "Well, at least I went to therapy and I tried to change." Her voice was shaking, too.

"And I am not anorexic!" Lori screamed to no one in

particular, because by that time her door was closed and no one was listening.

As she put her head in her pillow, Lori knew that she was anorexic.

Lori was shaking. That was a painful memory. She wasn't sure why it was worse than some of the others. The clock said 3:49, which meant her session had already gone four minutes overtime.

Dr. Wilson was looking at her earnestly. "You always have to stop and leave me hanging until the next time. How did you get out of the anorexia? Did you agree to go to therapy? Was that how you became a world-renowned anorexia specialist?"

Lori smiled. "It's fun sharing this with you, especially since you truly seem interested."

"I have to admit that sometimes when I listen to clients' stories, I get bored. I try my best not to feel that way, but you must know what I mean. However, I can tell you unequivocally that your story is totally spellbinding. Well, like it or not, I'll have to wait until next session. Do you still feel these sessions are productive?"

"Very much. I feel like a heavy load is being lifted off my body, slowly, slowly." Lori blushed. She liked it that yet again, Dr. Wilson seemed intrigued by her.

"That's good to hear. Enjoy your week."

Lori lifted her purse, gave a half smile, and walked out of the office.

CHAPTER 11

A s Lori pulled into Dr. Wilson's office parking lot, she popped a couple of aspirins into her mouth. Her head was throbbing. It had been a rough week. She'd fought with David often, and she couldn't figure out why. She was constantly annoyed with him these days, and David responded by criticizing everything she was doing. The therapy was supposed to be calming her down, but instead it seemed to be exacerbating her aggravation with her husband.

Lori thought intensely as she walked. David and the kids meant more to her than anything, absolutely anything. She was in therapy because she cared about them more than the oxygen she needed to live. She loved David. She truly did. He was extremely loyal and dedicated to her and their children. But that was only the beginning. Lori loved his passion for life and adventure. She loved his interesting insights into existence. She loved his single dimple on his left cheek. She loved his silly-sounding laugh. She loved his lopsided smile. She loved his deep blue eyes. She loved the delicate poetry he wrote for her and left under her pillow. She loved struggling through the challenges of their shared lives together. And if the initial spark was dwindling, she would do her best to stop it before it faded out completely...

Lori walked into the office building and took the elevator upstairs. She was early today. She had brought some work with her so she could catch up in the waiting room. She sat down on a chair, pulled out her laptop, and started to get to work. But she couldn't concentrate. Finally, the man who had the appointment before her exited Dr. Wilson's office. She looked at her watch. It was her turn.

"Hi, Lori," Dr. Wilson greeted her. "How was your week?"

"Not that great." She sighed and averted his gaze.

"Really?"

"Yeah. Nothing in particular. Just one of those weeks where everything seems negative."

Dr. Wilson turned his head slightly and waited for Lori to elaborate. But Lori just sat silently. She didn't feel like discussing her relationship with David or the petty arguments they had been getting into this past week. She valued her time here, where she could relive her past and ignore her present. She sat up straight and composed her thoughts.

"So, what's on the table for this week?" Dr. Wilson glanced at his notes, as if trying to remember where they had left off. "Oh, yes. Last week you were telling me about the time that you realized that you were anorexic." He seemed oblivious to the inner struggle that Lori was experiencing.

Lori, feeling relieved, nodded. She would much rather talk about this. She readjusted her thoughts and began.

"Yes, yes. That was at the end of my winter break during my sophomore year. Well, deep down I knew I had a big problem, but I kept convincing myself that I could stop it whenever I wanted. I also kept waiting and waiting for my parents to mention something themselves — without Hannah acting as their messenger. Yet they never said anything. They'd mutter things about how I was growing too thin and give each other looks, but they never questioned me directly."

"It sounds like you wanted them to say something."

"Very much. I wanted them to say, 'Lori, we're worried about you. Let's make an appointment with a psychologist. We want to help you.'"

"That would have showed you that they cared?"

"All those years when Hannah had all those psychological issues, all the help they gave her, all the time and money... I just wanted them to reach out to me, too." The bitterness in Lori's voice could not be concealed and she sniffled.

Dr. Wilson passed her the tissue box he had beside him. "It must have been hurtful."

Lori blew her nose and sighed deeply. She hated losing control of herself. But she loved feeling Dr. Wilson's empathy. She crossed her legs and continued, "I never understood. Why didn't they take the same initiative with me? Did they really not care that much?"

"Did you ever think that they may have seen you as more independent? That they respected your ability to help yourself more? From an outside perspective, it seems that way to me."

"Yeah, I guess so. But it was difficult all the same. By the time I returned to school, I was eating about four hundred calories a day. I weighed ninety-five pounds. At 5'6", I was obviously in trouble. I had no energy. I was having these terrible stomach pains and bloating problems. I kept saying that I was going to try to eat more, but I just couldn't do it. I was so scared that once I started eating more, I wouldn't be able to stop and before long, I would be fat."

"So, my million-dollar question: How did you get better?" Dr. Wilson looked up at the ceiling for a second. It was clear that he was contemplating something. "I guess I'm also curious from a professional standpoint."

Lori smiled softly. Again, she was able to intrigue Dr. Wilson.

Lori pulled up into the dorm parking lot and turned off the motor. How in the world would she get her suitcase into her room? Everything was taking way too much energy these days. She rested in the car for a few minutes. Finally, when she began shivering from the cold as the leftover heat wore off, she got out of the car. That was another problem these days — she was always freezing.

She pulled the suitcase out of the trunk, using every last bit of her strength. She dragged it up the path, bumping along some snow-covered patches. After what seemed like forever, she made it to the building. Luckily, her room was on the bottom floor and she wouldn't have to drag the suitcase upstairs.

Sophie was already back, sitting on her bed, reading. She looked up as Lori entered the room and smiled. "Hey. How was vacation?" Suddenly, her smile turned to a frown. "Lori, you look terrible. You lost even more weight."

Lori burst into tears. Sophie was a good friend, and her concern was valuable to Lori. All the pent-up emotion just exploded.

Sophie looked startled. "What's wrong?"

"I don't know. I think I need help. I don't feel good." Still crying, she collapsed on her bed.

"Look, Lori. Do you want me to take you to the emergency room?"

The panic in Sophie's voice helped Lori gain control again. She stopped crying. "No, I'll just make an appointment at the college clinic tomorrow morning."

Sophie accompanied Lori to the clinic the next day. The doctor looked at her history and did a brief exam. "You need to see a psychologist immediately," he said. He got Lori an appointment with a psychologist who specialized in eating disorders. The appointment was for that afternoon.

Lori went alone to the next appointment. She was feeling safer now that she knew there would be a professional taking responsibility for her.

She did not have to wait long to be seen; she was called in pretty quickly. The psychologist took some background information, weighed her, and took notes on her history. Then she left the room for a while.

When she returned, she told Lori that she had an eating disorder — she was demonstrating signs of anorexia and should really be admitted to a hospital immediately. Lori became hysterical and said she didn't want to go. The psychologist told Lori that she wanted to speak to her parents, but since Lori was an adult, she had to sign a consent form.

Lori refused to sign the papers and said she would be in charge of her own medical care. The psychologist got upset and said she could not help Lori if she was noncompliant. Lori calmed down and explained that she wanted to try therapy first. If that didn't work, she would agree to be admitted to a hospital.

The psychologist thought for a few minutes and then said, "Here's the deal. If you can gain five pounds by next week, I'll agree to see you without admitting you. If not, I'll only continue after you're admitted. I have liability and I can't risk something happening to you."

Now it was Lori's turn to think. Here she was. Alone. She had no one whom she trusted to ask advice, no one to guide her. She had never felt so alone in her life. She could look for another psychologist, but probably any psychologist would say the same thing. Besides, she didn't feel like waiting for tomorrow to get a new appointment.

Anorexic — it sounded scary. She was sick — psychologically. She knew that people could die of anorexia. Could she die? Help! She needed someone to help her! She felt desperate.

"I'll try it."

Lori went straight from her appointment to the library. She checked out any books on anorexia or eating disorders that she could get her hands on. For the next few days, she read and read.

Though she was desperate to gain some weight, it was almost like there was a metal wall between her and eating more than the four-hundred-calorie limit she had set. Still, there was one thing Lori was determined about — and that was not to be hospitalized. So eventually, she came up with a plan.

She had read that anorexia was often a control issue, so she decided she would trick herself. She would use this need for control in a positive way. If only she could convince herself that eating the exact amount — enough to be healthy, but not too much to become fat — would be the ultimate self-control, then maybe this need for control would actually help her recover.

Amazingly, it worked. Lori was able to increase her calorie intake enough that she gained four pounds by the next week. Although it wasn't the five-pound minimum set by the psychologist, the psychologist felt that Lori was not in as much danger and agreed to see her as a client.

"Wait a second. Your plan to cure yourself sounds familiar. Don't you do something like that in your clinic?" Dr. Wilson couldn't stop himself from interjecting.

Lori grinned. "I've developed this method scientifically. I based my PhD thesis on it, completed a large scientific study on it, and published numerous articles and a couple of books describing the successes of this method."

"I'm in awe. Was the psychologist you were seeing aware of what you were doing?"

"Not at all. She wasn't a bad psychologist, but she had some deficits. She used a complete cognitive-behavioral approach. She never did any psychoanalysis, never helped me come to terms with the reasons I felt so out of control, and never worked on resolving all my difficult family-relationship issues. Slowly, I began to recover, but a big part of my recovery was what I called 'self-therapy.' My recovery was a long process that took months and involved setbacks. But I was lucky. I always managed to maintain enough weight that I never had to be hospitalized. I took a lighter load of courses that semester, and amazingly I maintained my 4.0. I'd become very proud of my GPA. Probably another control thing.

"It was during this whole episode that I decided to change my major to psychology. I began dreaming of becoming a psychologist who specialized in eating disorders, and I began developing my now well-known method."

"Can you describe exactly how your method works?" Dr. Wilson looked somewhat sheepish. "Again, stop me if you want to stop this conversation. I know this doesn't relate to our therapy."

"Basically, all the therapists in my clinic use a strict structure for the sequence of therapy, which follows three basic steps. The first step involves getting our clients out of the danger zone. When our clients come in, they're usually in a severe state. Therapy doesn't work at this point, because starvation actually alters the rational side of the brain; there are numerous studies to support this. So our first goal is to get the client to a BMI that's high enough that therapy can be productive.

"Most hospitals and clinics use behavior-oriented approaches to accomplish this goal, offering rewards and privileges for weight gained. They monitor all food intake very carefully and don't even allow their patients to use the bathroom unmonitored — that's a privilege earned by gaining a certain amount of weight. This approach has always bothered me because here you are, taking people who have significant issues with needing to feel in control, and you're taking away even more of their ability to control any aspect of their lives. You're setting up a situation where the clients will try to sneak and get away with whatever they can — again, to maintain control of their own lives — in spite of outside influences trying to take away their control.

"That's why we take this very different and novel approach, in which the first step of our therapy is training our clients to use their need for control in a positive way, to get themselves to a healthy weight. We help them trick themselves, by making them realize that the ultimate control is to be a healthy size. We give them a challenge: Can they make themselves gain enough weight to be healthy, but not too much that they become fat? We build up the challenge, by saying that this actually takes a lot more control than what they are doing right now. We train our clients to use their incredible talent of self-control to help themselves get better. We respect all our clients and treat them that way.

"In the second step, once the client is at a healthier BMI, we use psychoanalysis to help the client understand and deal with the causes of this need for excessive self-control.

"Finally, in the third step, we help our clients find healthy ways to deal with control issues, positive outlets in which they can use this character trait in a good way.

"In the beginning, no one believed me that this method would work. However, our clinic is now world-famous. We have opened three similar clinics in other states and are considering branching out internationally."

"What are your fatality rates?" Dr. Wilson seemed to be pondering the possible effectiveness of this method.

"In our clinic here, we have not had a fatality — yet. Although there was one patient who committed suicide three years after leaving our clinic. I don't have to tell you this — when it comes to human behavior, there's no foolproof method. As much as I dream of having a 'fatality-free' clinic, I'm sure that we'll have our share of fatalities."

Dr. Wilson nodded slowly. "This has been very interesting to me. Thanks for sharing all that. I'd still like to take you up on your offer of meeting professionally; I have lots of specific questions that would be inappropriate for now. It's amazing what you've managed to create and develop based on your own experiences. I'm really inspired by you."

"As I said before," Lori replied, "just call my secretary and she'll set something up. And since our session is up, I'll see you next time."

Lori stood up abruptly. She had to hurry out today. David had a meeting and couldn't pick the kids up from school, so she had to rush back to get there on time. She looked directly at Dr. Wilson as she said goodbye.

CHAPTER 12

ALLISON HAD BEEN AT RAINBOW Clinic for a month now. It was clear to everyone that things were not going well. She had gained a pound the first week she'd been there, which had been great. But then all progress leveled off and she hadn't gained anything since then. She was weighing in at eighty-six pounds, a dangerously low BMI. The physician on staff told her that her electrolytes were off, her blood pressure was low, and she was at risk for cardiac arrest or renal failure.

Allison was scared. She didn't want to die. She just didn't want to live without anorexia.

She was acting just as she had acted in all previous therapy settings. During group therapy, she barely contributed. During individual therapy, she was "unengaged." During family therapy with her mom, she basically shrugged and nodded. She felt like everyone kept saying, "Allison, you have to engage more"; "Allison, we want to get to know you"; or "Allison, we can't understand you if you don't help us."

She didn't understand it herself. All those swirling thoughts in her brain. They twirled and wiggled, dove and spun, hurt and tickled — all at breakneck speed. It always seemed as though they were about to come hurtling out of her mouth. But then they banged. Smacked into a wall right at the edge of her brain. Right before they could get to her mouth.

She was now assigned an extra therapy session each morning. Her new therapist was Lori, one of the clinic's directors. That's how Allison knew things were really bad.

With all this said, and although Allison was aware that things were not going the way they should, she did not feel hopeless. She liked it at Rainbow Clinic. She was going to engage more. She was sure of it. She just needed more time. So nothing prepared her for the bombshell that was about to hit.

It was Monday morning. Weekends were downtime to relax, hang out with the other patients, or go on outings with family or friends. Structured therapy began again as the week started.

Allison checked her schedule. Nine thirty was her first therapy session of the day. She had Lori. At nine thirty sharp, Allison was sitting outside Lori's door. She had weighed herself earlier that morning at the weigh-in center, and was still at eighty-six pounds. She had nothing particular that she wanted to talk about. She wondered how Lori would direct the session.

The door opened. Lori popped her head out.

"Hi, Allison. Come in!"

Allison looked at Lori's slender figure. She wondered how she kept herself so thin at her age. Was *she* anorexic? Something about that made Allison feel mad. If she could work up the courage, she'd ask Lori about her own eating habits.

Allison walked in and sat down on the bright green chair. All the therapists' offices consisted of solid-colored furniture in all the rainbow colors. Lori was sitting on a yellow chair. There was a red desk pushed off to the side and a blue rug on the floor. The walls were painted in stripes of all the colors, although not in the ROYGBIV order.

"So, Allison, how was your weekend?"

Allison looked at Lori. She was smiling pleasantly. Allison wondered if she really cared. "It was okay."

"Did you do anything interesting?"

"No, not really."

"How are things going with the other patients here? Have you made any friends?"

Allison just shrugged.

"Do you have anything in particular that you'd like to discuss today?"

Allison raised one eyebrow and turned her head slightly. Again, she just shrugged her shoulders.

"Do you want to try to remember a dream you had last night? Maybe that will spark some memory about some other experiences."

"I never remember my dreams."

"Allison, you seem frustrated."

Allison stared out the window silently, although what she really wanted to say was, "Are *you* frustrated?"

"Don't be so hard on yourself about not gaining weight," Lori said. "Maintaining your current weight is actually safer for your health than gaining and losing patterns of fluctuating weight. Slow progress is much better. When you start recovering, you'll be more likely to maintain the progress. And just remember, you haven't lost any weight since you got here, which is progress in itself."

Allison continued sitting in stony silence. Her mind felt almost numb, her words trapped. Lori had gotten it all wrong. Allison wasn't disappointed by her lack of progress.

"You know, as I was reviewing your folder over the weekend, I realized that you never talked about your brother."

And then it happened. Without warning whatsoever. The brain waves that had been swirling around for months, trapped inside

Allison's head, suddenly pushed through. The wall came tumbling down.

"I don't want to talk about him! Who told you about him?! My mom told you, didn't she? She had to tell you! I hate her, I hate her, I hate her!!" Allison was clenching her jaw and her fists, and she was shaking.

Lori was staring at her like she was from another planet. "I'm so happy to see some emotion. But let's backtrack a little. I don't know what you didn't want your mother to tell me, but I can assure you that this had nothing whatsoever to do with her."

Allison breathed in deeply. This time, her voice was lower. "Then…how do you know about Will?"

Lori was still staring at her curiously. "On one of the reports, it mentioned that you had a brother, but I couldn't find any other mention of him. I thought that was strange. I also thought that it was strange that you've never talked about him before."

Once the wall had been broken, the thoughts just started pouring out. Allison was speaking loudly. "Okay, you want the whole story? I'll tell you the whole story. I made my mother promise not to mention my brother in any therapy session. And she agreed. She even said she understood. You know why?" She was talking so fast, it was hard to keep up.

"My whole life, everything has been about my brother. For once, I wanted this to be only about me. I wanted to pretend I never had a brother, that I was an only child. My whole life, my whole entire life, all I ever was, was a fly on the wall. A side point. When my brother was in second grade, he was diagnosed with ODD, oppositional defiance disorder.

"Before and after, my parents' lives have revolved around him. When he was eight, they put him in some sort of home. I was never allowed to see him or visit him. But he affected every aspect of my life. My parents were never available to me because they were always meeting with his doctors or therapists, visiting him, moving him to a new home, spending all their money on his treatments. Worst of all, their thoughts were always preoccupied with him. They never told me anything and still won't talk about him in front of me.

"And do you know what *I* was doing all this time? For all these years, I, their wonderful daughter, was being a good little girl. I followed all the rules. I got straight As on all my tests. I did all my homework without anyone reminding me. I made my bed every morning. I made my own lunches for school. And guess what? No one even noticed! I was a nobody.

"My parents gave up their lives for my brother, and where is he now? He's still in some home or maybe in a drug rehab center. They could've given me just a little bit of attention, and you know where I'd be now? Functioning normally. Maybe even on my way to a successful career. But they didn't, and I'm not.

"Do you know why I'm not 'progressing'? I'll tell you why." The words were cascading and tumbling out of Allison's mouth faster than she could think. She was expressing thoughts that she never knew existed inside her numb brain. "Because I don't want to get better! I don't want to die, but I don't want to go back to being a fly on the wall. Do you know that once I got sick, my whole life changed? Suddenly, I became the focus of my parents' lives! Now, they come with me to therapy. They spend the whole day trying to convince me to eat. They take me to doctors. They find programs for me. They're interested in me for the first time in my life! I never want to get better!!"

Allison finished speaking. Did those words really come out of her mouth? She covered her face with her hands and began to sob. She was crying for the first time in a long, long time.

Lori was just staring. Slowly, she came over to Allison and put her arm around her shoulders. Allison tensed up, but did not push Lori away.

"That was just what we've been looking for," Lori said. "That was great! You were so articulate, insightful, and mature in your understanding and expression of your innermost emotions."

Allison was slowly calming down. She looked up at Lori. Her eyes looked huge inside her shrunken face. The sadness inside them was almost unbearable to look at. Lori had to turn her gaze away.

"I may not want to live…but I don't want to die," Allison whispered.

"Allison, Allison. That's why you're here. And you just took a very big step on your road to recovery. Now, tell me some more about what it was like when you were a kid," Lori said, looking at Allison pleasantly.

And Allison talked and talked for almost an hour. They went over their session time, but Lori was so thrilled to hear the girl talk like this, that she almost felt like never ending the meeting. But finally, she had to stop it.

"Well, that was really interesting. I'm looking forward to hearing more tomorrow. You have an almost poetic way of expressing your thoughts. Have you ever written poetry?"

Allison blushed. Could Lori know about the secret stash of notebooks of poetry in which she wrote whenever she was feeling sad?

"Anyway, I think that the next step would be to get your mother involved. To talk about these feelings during family therapy time. Are you up for that?"

Allison shrugged nonchalantly, but felt her body tighten. "I guess it's okay, if you think that's a good idea."

"Don't worry," Lori said. "I'll be very tactful when I speak to your mother. I won't say anything that will make her upset."

Allison knitted her brows slightly. Talk to her mother? That was the last thing Allison wanted Lori to do. She tried not to panic. *No, no, no!* her insides were screaming. But she remained quiet and didn't say anything. Her shoulders sagged and her demeanor changed completely, but Lori didn't seem to notice.

Later that day, Allison was on a break, sitting in the lounge with some of the other girls. Suddenly, the door swung open and she saw her mother walking briskly toward her, her lips pulled tight. She looked like a wind-up toy that had just been wound up.

"Allison, I need to speak to you a minute." Her mother's voice appeared calm, but Allison could sense the ice dripping surreptitiously from the side.

Allison knew this had to do with Lori's conversation. Her heart started beating quickly. Her breaths were coming rapidly. She stood up and followed her mother out the door. Oh, why had she let Lori get her mother involved? Everything was going to be ruined now. Everything.

"Dear, I hope this won't come as a shock." Her mom put her arm on Allison's shoulder, but Allison shrugged it off.

"Just say what you want to say." Allison hated the suspense. Her mother always did that.

"You're going to need to pack up your bags. We're leaving here in a few hours."

Allison's eyes opened wide in surprise. "What?!"

"Don't get worked up. It's just that you've been here for a month, and our insurance won't cover it anymore. They have to see documentation of progress, and there's been none. There's nothing I can do. I wish it could work out, but there's no way that Dad and I can afford to pay for this privately."

Allison knew her mom was lying. She knew it as surely as she knew that her only friend left in the world, her only friend left, was anorexia. But she kept her thoughts to herself. What could she say? If she accused her mother of lying, she would just deny it. There was nothing she could do. Nothing except make her mother regret this decision for the rest of her life.

CHAPTER 13

LORI COULDN'T BELIEVE IT WAS November already. Only one month until the big event. She would have to talk to Dr. Wilson about more current issues if she wanted his help before she left on the trip. Lori had surprised herself by agreeing to go, and agreeing to take everyone along. Her mom and dad were happy, and so was David. She hoped that she had made the right decision.

It was good that Dr. Wilson had agreed to see her twice a week, so that she could get as much therapy time in as possible before December. This week, he had a cancellation and was giving her three appointments. She was making lots of progress, but she needed to make more. Let's see, she had been seeing him for over a month now; at two sessions a week, that must have been around ten sessions. Things were moving in the right direction.

As Lori sat down, Dr. Wilson stretched and then said, "Sorry, it's been a long morning."

Lori shrugged.

"How's everything going?" he asked.

"Well, did I mention that I've been arguing with my husband, David, a lot recently?" Lori blurted the words out, surprising herself. That must have been a good step. Did that mean that she was beginning to let herself admit her flaws?

Dr. Wilson shook his head and knitted his brow. "Why have you been arguing?"

"I can't figure it out. I feel perpetually annoyed at him. It's just odd. He's so kind, for the most part. But then, sometimes he gets resentful about something. He won't tell me what's wrong, but will act so cold. Everything will annoy him. I fight back, and then it seems like the whole day is constant petty bickering."

"So you think he's resentful about something, but you don't know what?"

Lori nodded.

"Well, I know very little about your personal life right now, so it's hard for me to figure out where to go with this."

Lori sighed. "I know. It's just that I have this need for you to understand my whole life before I get to what I need help with in the present."

Dr. Wilson looked at the ceiling and cracked his knuckles. "If we're going to continue in your past, how about answering this question: How did you meet your husband?"

Lori smiled. "Good idea." She paused again. "Last time, I ended the session by telling you how I began my road to recovery from anorexia. I had a couple of anorexia setbacks, but by the time I met David, I was pretty healthy. I had been involved in a serious relationship for a few months about half a year earlier. But the relationship had been rocky. The guy had some control issues. After we broke up, I was determined not to date anyone who was a controlling sort of person. When I met David, I was craving a deep friendship."

Lori was in her first year of a PhD program in neuropsychology at Columbia University. The work was intense, but she was enjoying it. She would frequent a bookstore with a coffee shop not too far from school. As she was sitting and drinking a coffee with a friend one morning, a guy approached their table.

"Hey!" he said to Lori.

"Do I know you?" Lori looked at him.

"No. But I've been watching you and I just wanted to tell you that I think the guy behind the counter likes you."

Lori rolled her eyes, but couldn't stop herself from turning around to see who was behind the counter. There was a cute, gangly guy, with longish auburn hair who was shrugging sheepishly. Lori recognized him. He often helped when she was buying coffee and was always very friendly. Nice guy. But not her type.

Lori turned back around and continued her conversation with Dana, a fellow student in her program. They finished up their coffees and got up to go. The guy from behind the counter called out to Lori, "Sorry about before. That was my friend Steve. He loves doing that to annoy me. It's just his way of playing a joke."

Lori looked up. "Don't worry about it."

"I'm David, by the way."

Lori smiled. "And I'm Lori"

"I've seen you around here before."

Lori really wanted to get back to school. "Yeah, I'm at Columbia. So this is a great little spot that's nearby."

"Well, I'm there, too. Maybe I'll see you on campus."

Lori gave a wave and headed out the door.

"Lori, he's cute!" Dana gave Lori a look.

"Oh, Dana, cut it out. I don't know anything about him." Lori started to blush. She wasn't sure why.

Over the next few weeks, Lori found herself visiting the coffee shop more and more often. Soon, she and David were old pals, joking and flirting with each other. Finally, David asked her out.

David was cute, smart, and completely chilled out. Lori loved his insights, his love of knowledge, and his relaxed lifestyle. He was getting a master's in English literature, but had no idea what he would do with that. Maybe teach. David played the guitar, loved reading, and refused to let anything or anyone pressure him. To Lori, there was something so refreshing about that.

Lori learned about David's family. He had a brother one year younger than he who wrote editorials. He had another brother who was at the University of California majoring in biochemistry. Lori felt like she could understand David.

David and Lori took a skiing trip during winter break. Lori had one of her best times ever. She'd always loved skiing since she had been a kid. It probably had to do with the fact that her family went on a skiing trip every couple of years, and while her dad loved skiing, Hannah hated it. So this was one of those rare situations in which Lori shared a special interest with her dad.

David and Lori's relationship was really solidified after that trip. Lori was officially in love. They dated the rest of that year. David was always kind and considerate. As a matter of fact, sometimes he was even so kind and considerate that it was annoying. But Lori was happy and secure in a way she had never felt before. Maybe this would be the man she would share her life with…

During the summer, Lori brought David home to meet her parents. They liked him. He seemed smart and knew how to act like a real gentleman. That finalized things in Lori's mind. Although she wasn't ready to admit it, she wanted to get married.

The next year during winter break, David and Lori planned another trip to a ski resort. David proposed while they were on a ski lift. Lori happily accepted.

Lori paused for a minute. "So that's how I met David."

"He sounds like a great guy."

"Yeah, I'm lucky. He's the kindest husband and father." Lori's tone was flat.

"You don't sound too convincing."

"Just sometimes, I wish he were more driven. He teaches high school and has no aspirations. He's a really talented writer. I'm always trying to convince him to write a novel. But he's totally happy taking the kids to the park, playing his guitar, having summers off. I can't relate to that." Lori didn't realize she felt this way until the words came tumbling out.

"Does he relate well to your kids?"

"Yeah, they're really attached to him. He has tons of patience and would probably be great if he were a stay-at-home dad. He's also insightful and really knows what the kids need." Lori wished she could be a great and dedicated mother, who matched David's abilities. But somehow, she just didn't have the patience that he had.

"Does it bother David that you are so driven?"

"How could it bother him? I make a lot of money for our family and I'm successful." Lori turned a little pink as the irony of what she was saying dawned on her. She looked at Dr. Wilson, who was knitting his brows at her. Then she spoke in a quieter voice. "Wow, that came out sounding funny. I guess the bottom line is that sometimes I'm jealous of David." She couldn't believe those words had just escaped her lips. Her cheeks turned pinker and burned hotly.

"Lori, it's great to hear you admit to some negative feelings, to something that may have been hard to acknowledge." Dr. Wilson sounded genuinely impressed, which detracted from the shame Lori was currently feeling. She tried to focus on feeling pride in admitting non-flattering aspects of her psyche, even though this was just the tip of the iceberg.

Dr. Wilson waited. When Lori did not add anything, he continued, "It seems to me that in your very controlled life, with your super-achieving nature — and don't get me wrong; you've done great things with those very qualities — you found some sense of relief, some eye-opening freedom in David's very carefree living. You are attracted to it and admire it. Maybe sometimes you're jealous of it. And sometimes it just irks you that he lives so differently than you. But I think that deep down — and even not so deep down — you like those differences, like the balance it brings to your life."

Lori nodded vigorously as Dr. Wilson talked. Yes, he had articulated that perfectly. She smiled and then sighed deeply. David was so different from her. But she was lucky. He was a good man, and he did help her live a more balanced lifestyle.

Again, Dr. Wilson waited. But Lori was deep in thought. So he asked another question. "Did Hannah ever get married?"

"Now that's a whole different story." Lori was glad to change the subject.

Dr. Wilson turned slightly and lifted his eyebrows.

"At first, Hannah really enjoyed her work at MIT. She made some exciting discoveries, came up with a theory, and published all her work together with her mentor, the professor who had hired her. She was building up a name for herself in the science world. But then things began to grow complicated in her relationship with her mentor. I think she wanted more autonomy. Also, she felt like he was taking credit for work that she was doing. At least that was what I was able to piece together from the information that my parents shared with me.

"Finally, she left and took a position as a professor at Yale. At this point, she'd won some prestigious science awards and was building her acclaim. I wasn't talking to her that often, but from the snippets I heard from my parents she seemed to be doing well emotionally, too. Then I heard from my parents that she was dating a professor whom she worked with. My parents sounded excited about the guy. He was some sort of science genius, too.

"But then I began to hear updates from my parents that sounded pretty bad. It seemed that their relationship was volatile and explosive. They were getting into horrible fights, and Hannah would call my parents crying hysterically. She was back to some of her old behaviors. About a month before my wedding, Hannah ended the relationship. In an unexpected move, she called me to tell me that she was no longer dating her boyfriend. I'm still not sure why she wanted to talk to me about it, but we ended up having a pretty interesting discussion."

Lori was sitting at the table in her apartment with a list of things to do before the wedding. Finals were next week, and then the wedding would be three weeks later, on June 17. She hoped it wouldn't be too hot. The phone was ringing, but she really had no patience to answer it. On the fourth ring, she changed her mind and picked up the receiver.

"Hello?"

"Hi, Lori. It's me, Hannah."

"Hi." Lori was caught slightly off guard. Hannah rarely called just to say hello, so something must be going on.

"How're all your wedding plans going?"

"I think well." She wanted to tell Hannah to just get to the point already, but she bit her lip and waited patiently.

"That's good. Oh, I just wanted to tell you that you can take Marshall off your list of guests. I moved out of his apartment. We broke up."

"Yeah, Mom mentioned something about that. How are you doing?"

It was odd. Hannah seemed to want to talk about it.

"Not that bad." Another awkward pause.

Lori wasn't sure what to say next. "Do you think you guys may ever get back together?" Now that was a dumb question, and Lori realized that the minute she said it.

"Absolutely not," Hannah answered. "As a matter of fact, I've had an epiphany."

"What's that?"

"Well," Hannah said, "don't take any of this the wrong way. These are totally personal decisions."

"Don't worry." Lori rolled her eyes to no one in particular.

"I have come to the conclusion that I am not going to get married."

"Ever?"

"Ever."

"Hannah, don't say that! Just because you had one bad experience, you can't give up."

"No, it's much deeper than that. It's just something I've realized about myself."

"And that is?" It was hard to talk to Hannah. Lori had to drag the information out of her.

"Look, I was born with certain unique talents. I have the ability to change the world. To discover things. To help humanity for generations to come. I realized while dating Marshall that I can't be successful in a relationship, in developing a family, and also devote the time and energy that's required to produce the theories and research that I'm capable of. The way I see it, I can help create one family or help save billions of families."

"Don't say that. Many scientists find a way to make both work. I'm sure you can do it."

"No, I am sure that I cannot. The family lifestyle just doesn't fit with my current or future lifestyle." Hannah stopped and then suddenly added, "But don't worry. I'm not judging your decision to get married. Not everyone has unique talents that can actually save mankind."

Lori clenched her teeth and told herself she would not even respond to that comment. Hannah didn't mean to be insulting. As absurd as it was, Hannah thought that she was being sincere.

"Isn't it crazy that she could make a comment like that? Hannah's social skills are so warped."

Dr. Wilson nodded. "And I take it she kept to her word and never married?"

"Yes, she never married. And never developed any significant relationship with a man again, to the best of my knowledge."

"How did your parents feel about this?"

"Interesting question. I think they would have been happy if she would've married. However, they idealized her brilliance and protected it. And I think they felt that nothing should get in its way, just like Hannah felt."

Dr. Wilson sat up straight and closed his folder. "Well, Lori, it's been another interesting session. Looking forward to our next one."

"Thanks," said Lori, as she got to her feet. "See you next time."

CHAPTER 14

THE RAIN WAS REALLY COMING down hard. Lori sat in her car for a moment, wishing it would stop. However, it was obvious that it wasn't stopping anytime in the near future and her appointment was in three minutes. She was caught off guard, with no raincoat and no umbrella. So she swallowed hard, opened the car door, and made a dash for the building. She wasn't parked so far from the door, but she was drenched by the time she got inside. Now what? She shook herself off and rummaged through her purse. Finding a rubber band, she pulled back her dripping hair into a ponytail. She smiled at the security guard, who had been watching her since she entered the building. Then she headed into the elevator.

"It must be pouring out there." Dr. Wilson looked at Lori's brown blouse, which was plastered to her body, and raised his eyebrows, chuckling.

Lori laughed. "Yes, I was not prepared for it."

Dr. Wilson walked over to the window and peered out. "I'm happy that I'm sitting in here right now!"

Lori reached for a tissue and wiped her face.

"I used to love rain as a kid. Something about the pounding sound of the rain hitting the windows and the comfort and security of sitting cozily inside." Dr. Wilson was nostalgic.

"Yeah, I know what you mean." Lori thought for a moment. "I

loved rain, too. Hannah, on the other hand, hated rain as a kid. She had some sort of phobia of floods. Whenever it was raining, even if it wasn't a thunderstorm, she had to sleep in my parents' bedroom. There was one year when she wouldn't even go out of the house when it was raining. She must have been nine. If it was ever raining in the morning, my father would have to carry her, kicking and screaming, to school."

"Wasn't she afraid of swimming?" Dr. Wilson recalled an old memory that Lori had shared.

"Yeah, Hannah had a fear of water and never learned how to swim. For a while, my parents tried really hard to help her overcome it. But then they just gave up. You know, as I'm thinking about this, I'm realizing that a lot of Hannah's research at MIT and at Yale has been on water. I wonder if this is a coincidence, or if there is some subconscious relationship."

"Did Hannah have any other phobias?"

"Now that you ask, Hannah had this really absurd phobia of windup toys. If she saw one, she'd go crazy, screaming, holding her head, squeezing her eyes shut. It was really embarrassing."

"Embarrassing for you?"

"Well, a couple of times it happened when I had friends around. I was mortified."

"Do you have any phobias?"

"Well, I used to get panic attacks whenever I was stuck in traffic. But I've gotten much better. Also, I don't like flying, but I do it anyway." Lori sat back in her seat, indicating she was ready to start.

"So back to where we left off last time." Dr. Wilson took her cue, removing his glasses as he spoke and wiping them on his shirt. Then he put them back on and took out his notes. "You were telling me about the time right before your wedding."

"Yes, things worked out quite well, actually. The wedding was relatively smooth. No major disasters, no big fights. I was sure that Hannah would pull some stunt, go into some massive depression or something to take away my parents' attention on this special day of mine, but she didn't. She showed up at the wedding, and actually gave a nice toast. My parents seemed really happy, and David's family did, too. It was a fun day."

"So your relationship with Hannah improved?"

"I wouldn't say that. We had minimal contact for the next ten years or so. We'd call each other every couple of months. We never had that much to talk about. The next big fight with Hannah didn't happen for some years, though."

"What caused this fight?"

"Well, after David and I married, we began to settle into our lives. I had two more years until I completed my PhD. I was working on my thesis and doing fellowship hours. David graduated right before our wedding, so he began work at a high school near where we were living. Things were moving along. After I graduated, I got a great job working for a well-known psychologist who specialized in eating disorders. My thesis had been published in a psychology journal and this guy read it, liked it, and wanted me to work for him.

"I did that for two years, at which point the psychologist I was working for got a job as a professor in an Ivy League school. He was older and happy to retire from his practice, so he offered to sell it to me. I bought it, along with two partners I'd developed professional relationships with. Since these partners also specialized in eating disorders, we changed it into a clinic that only saw clients with eating disorders. We were fortunate that it was successful from the get-go. We were filling a much-needed niche. Pretty soon, we had to move to a larger facility as our clinic continued growing and growing.

"At this point, I was thirty-three. David was ready to start a family, but I didn't feel like the time was right yet. I wanted things to be more stable with my business, so that I could take some time off when I had a kid and not worry about everything falling apart.

"David would bring up the subject of kids everyone so often, but I would just brush him off. We bought a house in the suburbs that was kid friendly. David moved to a better school where he taught tenth- and eleventh-grade English and literature. He also formed a band with a group of friends. They played at different bars on weekends. At this point, my clinic was huge. I traveled a lot, giving lectures and workshops. We were doing well financially, too.

"Before I knew it, it was my thirty-sixth birthday, and David became more assertive about starting our family. He felt like we were running out of time. I agreed, so finally I was ready. We tried to get pregnant that whole year. But we were unsuccessful. After a comprehensive exam by my ob-gyn, in which he found nothing notable, we decided to take some fertility drugs to try to help things along. By then I was thirty-seven. If that didn't work, we would have to take more drastic steps, such as looking into the possibility of IVF. Time was running out.

"I had this nagging worry that I had messed up, putting so much focus on my business. What if I had ruined our chances of having a child? I would have been devastated. And I would have felt even more horrible that I ruined David's chances. I knew how badly he wanted a child. But we were lucky and that was not to be. Three months later, I learned that I was pregnant. David and I were ecstatic.

"We went for a sonogram at ten weeks, just to make sure every-thing was normal. We were shocked when the technician casually told us to look at the two fetuses! She had assumed we knew that we were expecting twins, when in fact, we had not. I can vividly recall looking at David as we both started laughing and crying at the same time. We were excited for many reasons, but especially since we knew that I probably would not want to get pregnant again at forty, so now we could have the two kids we wanted without having to go through the whole pregnancy thing again.

"Of course, there were many concerns, too, like hoping the ba-bies would be healthy, as well as the physical challenges of having two infants at once! We called family members to tell them the news. Everyone was ecstatic, just like we were. My parents obvi-ously had no grandchildren yet. David's parents had two grandsons and one granddaughter, but since we live the closest to them, only a forty-five-minute drive, this was going to be extra exciting.

"But when I spoke to Hannah, my conversation with her went pretty poorly."

Lori unlocked the front door and walked into their house. She was exhausted. This pregnancy thing was not easy. She had thrown up three times this morning at work. She'd been in a session with a client, and she had to keep excusing herself so she could go to the restroom to puke. That was not fun! The good thing was that she was eleven weeks pregnant, so the morning sickness was not supposed to last much longer.

Lori grabbed a water bottle from the refrigerator and a stack of crackers, which sometimes helped with the nausea, and col-lapsed on the couch. David's school had a big football game that night, so he would be home late. She closed her eyes and drifted into a brief sleep. She started dreaming about crying babies and flying strollers.

Suddenly, the ringing phone brought her back to the present. She sat up and rubbed her eyes. There was a phone on the coffee table next to her. Groggily, she picked it up.

"Hello?" Lori tried not to sound tired.

"Hi, Lori. It's me, Hannah."

"Hi, Hannah! How are you? I'm guessing Mom and Dad told you the exciting news." Lori felt a little awkward, but she was not sure why.

"Yes, that's why I'm calling. I wanted to wish you congratulations."

"Thanks!"

"Are you feeling well?"

"Pretty good. You must have heard that we're expecting twins."

"Yes. Double the excitement, huh?"

"We have a lot to do to get ready."

"When are you due?"

"March 14."

"Maybe I'll come down after the babies are born."

"That would be great. You can finally see our house."

"Anyway, I just wanted to give you a little advice. Do you mind?"

Lori felt annoyed already. She wanted to say, "No, thank you," which would have been the smarter move, but instead she said, "Sure."

"You know, I'm very proud of all the great work you've been doing in your research on eating disorders. You're really building a reputation for yourself."

Interesting. Lori didn't even realize that Hannah knew what she did. "Thanks," she said flatly. She did not like where this conversation was going.

"So I just want to advise you not to get too caught up in the excitement of having new babies, that you take off a lot of time from work or lose your focus."

"Really?" Lori felt her blood bubbling. Who was Hannah to tell her this? Hannah, the expert at juggling family and work!

"Really. I've seen it happen to the best scientists. Once they have kids, they're no longer able to focus on their work. That's it. It's the end of their career. I've even known some who never went back to work."

Lori was almost exploding. Hannah had no clue that Lori was already plagued with guilt that her career had almost destroyed her chances of having children.

"Well, you know what? I respect those women!" Lori said. "I think that raising children is a very valuable job."

"I'm not saying that raising children is not a valuable job. A woman just has to weigh the value of what she's accomplishing against the value of what she can achieve by staying home with her children."

Leave it to Hannah to make it all about weighing percentages of values, ignoring the emotional aspects. Lori was trying to stay calm, but it was almost impossible. Wasn't this crazy? Hannah never called, never initiated dialogue, and suddenly she felt this need to advise her!

"I'm sorry, but I don't agree. I think that raising children is the most valuable job there is!" Lori was using extremes, but Hannah had pushed her to her limit.

"Are you telling me that raising children is more valuable

than my research into decreasing drought in the world, which has the potential to save billions of lives?!" Something Lori had said hit a nerve in Hannah. Now Hannah sounded livid.

"Yes! And you know what? Next time, keep your insane advice to yourself. I'm not interested in your absurd thoughts!" Lori had a lot more things she wanted to say.

"Fine! I will. Enjoy the kids. Don't come crying to me when everything you've built up is destroyed. I thought you surprised us all by turning out smart. I guess it wasn't true, after all."

Lori slammed down the phone. She was shaking uncontrollably. At that moment, she hated Hannah with all her being.

Dr. Wilson looked at Lori with those piercing eyes that always seemed to be reading deep into her. She turned away.

"Did you ever make up after that conversation?"

"No. I didn't talk to Hannah for the rest of the pregnancy. After the twins were born, she tried to call to wish me congratulations, but I wouldn't talk to her. She sent a gift — two cute toys. She was definitely trying." Lori leaned back in her seat.

"But the worst part was that soon after I had the babies, she came down with another one of her episodes. My mother-in-law stayed with us for a couple of weeks after the babies were born to help out. My parents were supposed to come and see them the next week. But then Hannah had a breakdown and had to move back home for a few months. She took off the semester from teaching. My parents were back to taking care of her full-time. I switched off from feeling intense anger that once again she took my parents from me at a time when I needed them, to feeling horrible guilt that maybe our argument sparked this episode."

"So your parents didn't come to see the babies?"

"When they were one month old, my dad came alone for three days. Then he went back and my mom came. I was so mad that my adult sister made one of my parents stay home with her, and so mad that my parents went along with it! I finally had children, my parents were finally grandparents, and I couldn't enjoy it with them." As she spoke, Lori raised her voice without meaning to.

"Did your parents ever express remorse that they couldn't be with you as much as they would have wanted?"

"No." Lori frowned. "I wish they would have. I think that would've made it a little better."

"So, wait. What did you have? Were the twins girls or boys?"

Lori smiled. "A girl and a boy. Emma and Matthew." She reached into her purse and pulled out a photo.

Dr. Wilson looked at the photo closely. Emma was smiling almost mischievously. She had long blond curls pulled back in a pony and bright brown eyes that were wide and full of life. Matthew had wavy brown hair, two adorable dimples, and dark chocolate-colored eyes. He had a serious expression on his face and was looking past the camera. "They're adorable." He looked up at Lori and then back to the photo again. "Neither of them looks like you."

"I know. Emma looks like my husband, except for the hair. She has my hair. And Matthew — people actually think he looks like Hannah. Strange, no?"

"That is strange. How old are they?"

"They're five now, in pre-K. I can't believe they'll be in kindergarten next year."

"Well, I'd love to hear how you ended up balancing parenting and work, but we're already five minutes overtime."

"I'll tell you about that next time."

As Lori headed out of the office, she glanced out of a window.

She was relieved to see that the rain had stopped and the sun was shining.

CHAPTER 15

ALLISON HAD BEEN BACK AT home for four days now, and things had gone from bad to disastrous. During the plane ride home, she had closed her eyes and tried to sleep. But instead of sleeping, she watched little men in her brain work hard to slowly fix the wall that had broken in Lori's office the last day at Rainbow Clinic.

When she'd arrived home, Allison had barely acknowledged her father's warm welcome. She climbed straight into bed. She flat out refused to eat anything. This time, she was not even pretending to eat. She lay in bed all day, also refusing to talk to anyone. On her third day home, her father came into her room with a tray of her favorite foods. Allison wouldn't even look at him.

Finally, he started screaming at her. "This is my house, and in my house you will follow my rules. If you want to live here, you have to eat. Otherwise, get out!" Allison was so sick, she barely heard him. She was in another world. Her thoughts were floating hazily. She could barely catch them, let alone know what they were.

Allison's mother heard her father screaming and came into the room. She started screaming back, "Are you out of your mind?! Our daughter is one sick girl and you're telling her you're going to kick her out of our house?!"

"You're right. I'm telling her that I will kick her out! She can make herself eat a little. You can't convince me that she has no control over herself. And I have a right to make rules around here and expect my kid to follow them!"

"Yeah, well, if all the doctors and all the therapists couldn't get her to eat, you think your stupid rule is going to get her to eat?!"

"What do you want me to do — just sit here and watch my daughter starve herself to death like you seem to be doing?! You've been making most of her therapy decisions until now, and they don't seem to be working. I'm going to do things my way for a change!"

Allison's parents continued yelling. She curled up into a ball, closed her eyes, and tried picturing a beautiful garden with blue jays and monarch butterflies, with tulips and daffodils. It was hard. The only picture she was able to visualize was an empty patch of land with dark, thorny vines, desolate and barren. Finally, her parents left the room.

The next morning, Allison's father came back into her room. "Allison, you have to get dressed. We're taking you back to the hospital." He was talking calmly.

Allison shuddered, but had no energy to even argue. Her father helped her change out of her pajamas, which were starting to smell, and put on a clean sweatshirt and sweatpants. He winced noticeably as he saw her ribs and hip bones protruding out of her tightly drawn skin.

Her skin was pulled so tight it was almost translucent. Her hip bones were so pointy they almost looked like sharp daggers. Her stomach was swollen like pictures of starving kids in Africa. Allison tried to ignore her father's looks. She was so weak she could barely stand, so her father lifted her up and carried her to the car, where her mother was already waiting. It felt nice to be held. When she closed her eyes, she felt like she was a baby back in her daddy's arms. Like he could pick her up and hold her tight and protect her from all the world's troubles.

They drove in stony silence. Allison was not talking because she literally had no strength to move her mouth. Her parents weren't talking because they had nothing to say. She could feel her parents' despair.

They arrived at the hospital and had Allison checked into the children's unit. She weighed in at seventy-seven pounds. Her body temperature and blood pressure were dangerously low. Without intervention, her heart was likely to stop beating in the next few days. She was dehydrated, too. An IV drip was started immediately to help with rehydration. Allison had mixed feelings about the IV. She knew it was pumping calories into her body. She wanted it out, but not badly enough to fight. And she was so scared of dying that a tiny bit of her brain told her to acquiesce.

A few hours later, Allison was still lying in her hospital bed. She had no interest in interacting with anyone and would not respond or make eye contact. She just lay in bed, staring at the ceiling, trying her best not to think. Her parents sat on two chairs, resting and reading some magazines, waiting to talk to a doctor.

Finally, after what seemed like an eternity, a doctor and a psychiatrist entered the room and began talking with her parents. Allison lay there listening, angrier than ever that no one was including her in the conversation. She heard them talk about inserting the dreaded feeding tube. She heard them explain that force-feeding her at this point would have no long-term benefits, but it may be necessary to get her out of this danger zone, and to get her to have enough strength to start therapy again.

Allison wanted to scream, wanted to tell them they had no right to insert a feeding tube — to invade her body without her permission. But she just lay there listlessly, like a log floating down a river at the mercy of the current. On one hand, it seemed like gaining back any control in her life was as insurmountable as building a Great Wall of China single-handedly. On the other hand, there was one thing that she had perfect control over, and she would never give that up: her fight against food.

The next thing Allison knew, a nurse was wheeling a cart into her room to begin the simple procedure of inserting a nasogastric tube. She felt like a time bomb waiting to explode. Maybe, just maybe, if the doctors had talked to her, explained the necessity to her… Maybe, just maybe, if they would have asked her permission… If they would have reminded her that she didn't want to die…maybe she would have agreed. But to breach her privacy so blatantly, to invade her body so intrusively, to force her to do the one thing she had control over… *Never.* She would not allow it.

The nurse began explaining the procedure, telling Allison that it would be the easiest if she remained calm. Suddenly, Allison was screaming. The monster inside had awoken again. "Get out! Get out!! Don't you dare touch me!!" she yelled, while kicking and flailing her arms.

The nurse was taken by surprise. Allison's feet knocked the cart over. The nurse just stared at her in shock and then left the room. In a minute, a doctor and a group of nurses were there. One nurse took out a shot and suddenly everything went black.

When Allison woke up, she felt the tube in her nose. She tried to reach for it to yank it out, but her arms wouldn't move. She glanced to her side and saw that her arms were in restraints. She looked around the room. It was dark outside. Her dad was asleep in the chair and her mom was gone. Allison felt like her insides were on fire. How did the doctors have permission to do this? How did her parents let them do this? She was as angry as she had ever been. She felt like a volcano spewing lava. The only difference was that her volcano was silent. She wondered if she could get a lawyer and sue the hospital.

Allison was exhausted. She felt her eyes drooping but didn't fight it. She let herself drift off into a deep sleep.

≈

Over the next few days, Allison's mom and dad took turns sitting with her, while she refused to talk to anyone. The doctors, always talking about Allison in front of her, like she was deaf or mentally limited, said that this was okay. The goal was to let the feeding tube slowly help her gain back some weight, until she would be out of immediate danger and more mentally competent to be involved in therapy. They advised her parents to just be supportive and loving for the next week or so. Allison seethed silently.

It was six days later. Allison's mom was sitting beside her, in silence.

"Allison, I'm going down to the gift shop to buy something. Is there anything you want?"

Allison just bit her lip and stared at the wall.

"Oh, why do you have to make this so difficult?" her mom muttered.

Allison saw a couple of bricks fall off the wall in her brain. And then she started talking. "Me? Make this difficult for you? It's you who has made this so difficult for me! What do you think you're doing, allowing the doctors to force this tube down my throat and keep my arms in restraints? You think you're going to force me to get better? You think you can force me to be however you want, just like you did my whole life?" Though her voice was shaking, she was speaking calmly and quietly.

Her mom was hurt. It was apparent in her eyes. "Allison, no matter what you say, I love you more than anything. What do you expect me to do? Just sit here and watch you slowly die?" Tears started streaming down her face. "If this is the only way for me to keep you alive, then I will do what I have to. I am not losing you!"

"Yeah, well, if you really wanted me to get better, you would've let me stay at Rainbow Clinic. If you heard one word they said there in all the workshops and therapy sessions, you'd know that for any chance of long-term recovery, I have to buy into it. I have to feel like I'm in control of the process. You can't think you'll force me to get better and it'll work!"

"Oh, don't bring any proofs from that scam of a place!" Allison's mom stopped crying, and her voice turned angry. "They have no clue what they're doing there. They should be shut down before they scam more innocent victims. They're the ones who turned you against me!"

Allison breathed in deeply. She turned away and shut her eyes. She almost stopped talking. But then she turned around again. "You just can't deal with it, because Lori finally told you something that hit home. You can't handle the guilt. So you pulled me out and resorted to the only thing you know how to do — force me to do what you want. Well, it won't work. You can't keep this feeding tube in me indefinitely. You'll never force me to get better if I don't want to." Allison's voice was icy cold.

"Please don't say those horrible things," her mother begged. "Why don't you believe me? I really love you!"

But Allison turned away again and refused to talk anymore. She was done.

CHAPTER 16

LORI COULD NOT BELIEVE THEY would be leaving in three weeks. There was so much to do before the big trip. Her gown had to be altered; David's and Matthew's tuxedos had to be picked up; Emma's gown was ready, but she needed shoes; Lori needed shoes, too. Then Lori had to make sure they all had enough dressy clothes for the rest of the week. In addition, there was all the arranging for while they were away: the mail, the dog, the clinic. And, of course, packing.

Right now, it seemed totally overwhelming. Lori hoped she'd made the right decision about going. And about bringing Emma and Matthew.

She turned into the parking lot, her mind in constant motion, trying to schedule all she had to do. She hurried out of the car and into the office.

"Good afternoon." Dr. Wilson gave Lori a big smile.

"Hi." Lori barely smiled.

"You seem stressed out."

"Just a lot to take care of."

"Do you want to talk about it? Or continue as usual?"

Lori thought for a moment. "I guess I'd like to continue." She inhaled slowly.

"Well, if I remember correctly, you were about to tell me about juggling motherhood and working. Hannah had thought it would be challenging. I'm curious how you pulled it off."

Lori raised her eyebrows and gave Dr. Wilson a look. Then she shrugged and started speaking.

"When the twins were born, I officially took a four-month maternity leave. I sold some of my ownership of the practice so that I was down to twenty percent ownership (while my other two partners each had forty percent ownership) and did not have to be as involved in the everyday running of it. However, unofficially, I continued helping out with a lot of the management. Even though I wasn't going to work every day, I went into the clinic a few times a week to oversee some things and meet with the staff. If any big decisions had to be made, I would come in for meetings. It was too hard not to be involved.

"By the time the twins were four months old and my maternity leave was drawing to a close, I was itching to be on a regular work schedule again. We found a nanny, and I went back to work four days a week.

"We're lucky that David has such a great schedule. Since he follows the school calendar, he has lots of vacation time, he's off in the summer, and gets home by three thirty every day except Monday. That's helped a lot. Things have worked out pretty well. Although, I have to admit, I'm always feeling guilty."

"Guilty about working?"

"Guilty about working too much and guilty about not working enough. You know, I sometimes regret that I could never be fully devoted to work like I had been before the babies were born. I'm worried that I'm not giving my clients the devotion they need. On the other hand, I always feel that I'm not around enough as a mother, that my mind is on other things, that I can't devote myself to my kids the way they need me to."

"So was Hannah right, after all?"

"No!" Lori said, a little too emphatically. "I mean, I wouldn't give up motherhood for anything, and if I had to pick one over the other, I would choose being a parent to having a career, hands down. Hannah had a point, but I think she got it backward." Lori paused. "I think this dilemma has been the plight of women in recent years. We try so hard to be great at both our careers and parenting, which is an almost impossible task. At the end of the day, a woman can feel dissatisfied with both."

"Does that mean you believe women who want to have kids should not work?"

"No. I mean — I'm not sure what I think. I believe women have so much to offer the world through their careers. And on a personal level, staying home all day can be a frustrating experience. I think many women would not be satisfied with that either, and that's ignoring the financial aspects. On the other hand, kids need their parents. I think they need at least one parent, either the mom or the dad, to be totally devoted to taking care of their needs, especially in the early years. It's complicated and I haven't worked out the perfect solution yet."

"I think I'd go out of my mind if I were a stay-at-home dad." Dr. Wilson let out a little chuckle.

"I don't think I'd be so good at it myself," Lori replied. "But David, on the other hand, would be great at it. He's shown me how stimulating being a parent can be. He's always doing things with the kids, teaching them, showing them things. He has endless patience. They're lucky to have him as a dad."

"Did he ever seriously consider becoming a stay-at-home dad?"

"He wanted to, but I kept vetoing it."

"For financial reasons?"

"No. I was doing well enough that it wouldn't have had a tremendous impact on our lives if he stopped working. He could have made some extra money tutoring. And we would've saved a lot of money on day care."

"So why didn't you guys do it? I certainly admire someone who can do that."

Lori looked at Dr. Wilson. "I don't know why I was so resistant."

Dr. Wilson turned his head slightly and waited.

"Maybe it's that laid-back personality thing that drove me crazy. It felt weird that he wouldn't have any structure. That he wouldn't be *doing* anything. It just seemed so lazy!"

"You think David is lazy?"

"No. I can't explain it." Lori hesitated. "It just seems that David is never pushing himself to accomplish things. And this played into that feeling."

"Didn't you say that being a stay-at-home parent is challenging? And didn't you say that David has taught you how to be a parent in a stimulating way? If someone can do it successfully, that seems like a huge accomplishment."

"Yes, you're right." Lori got lost in thought for a few moments. Dr. Wilson wrote some notes as he waited.

Lori looked up again. "You once mentioned you have sons. How many do you have? Do you also have girls?" Lori knew she was crossing a line and perhaps asking a question that was inappropriate, but she'd let Dr. Wilson stop her if he chose not to answer.

"Just three boys! It's pretty wild."

Lori glanced around the office. No pictures. Oh, well.

Dr. Wilson watched her. "I'll bring you a photo next time," he said.

"You always seem to read my mind!" she exclaimed.

Dr. Wilson shrugged. "That's my job: understanding people, including their verbal and nonverbal communication."

"I'm continually gaining respect for your abilities. You have a subtle style that has allowed me to articulate and express thoughts I've kept bottled inside me for many years."

"From you, that's truly a compliment."

An awkward silence filled the room. "So, we left off with Hannah in another bad state living back at home and your relationship in shambles," Dr. Wilson said, breaking the ice.

"That's a good way to put it. Yeah, Hannah stayed at my parents through the summer. David and I wanted to bring the kids for a short visit before I started work again, but my parents felt like it wouldn't be a good time. Hannah wouldn't come out of her room and apparently was having suicidal thoughts. My parents were horribly worried."

"I'm sure that was another disappointment."

"Yeah, it just wasn't fair. I wanted my kids to have grandparents who cared about them. Finally, I thought I had something to offer them that Hannah didn't have: grandchildren. But it didn't make a difference. It was painful."

"When was the next time your parents visited you and the twins?"

"My parents actually came down for a week that September. That was a nice memory." Lori smiled. "My dad and mom had a lot of fun playing with Emma and Matthew. I felt better after that visit."

"And what about Hannah?"

"Once again, Hannah seemed to slowly pull herself out of the mess she was in. She went back to Yale for the fall semester, but I was getting the impression she wasn't happy there anymore. Something about changing her research focus. Right before winter break, she accepted a position at Berkeley, but it wouldn't begin until the following year. I called Hannah to congratulate her on the position. It was sort of my way of making up with her. It was a brief, awkward conversation. Hannah asked about the kids. They were ten months at that point. I told her that I was considering making a big one-year-old bash, inviting relatives and friends. Hannah said she would consider coming. I thought that was a nice offer, but I have to admit, I was worried that she would somehow ruin it."

"So did she come?"

"Of course not!" Lori said bitterly.

Lori mailed out all the invitations for the birthday party early that morning. It was Friday and she usually did not go into work on Fridays. She had devoted this day to making arrangements for the party. It would be on a Sunday in two and a half weeks. Lori and David had decided to make this a family and friend get-together, a celebration of the joy they felt in having Emma and Matthew. It would be more of an adult affair, although kids were invited. They were having a brunch in their home and Lori was really looking forward to it. David's parents were coming, of course — they came to visit most Sundays — but Lori's parents were coming, too, which Lori was excited about. Aunts, uncles, cousins, colleagues, and neighbors were also invited.

Lori strapped the kids into their car seats. Matthew started crying. He always hated the car. She hoped this wouldn't be too much — going shopping with both kids. She could have waited until Monday and left a little early from work, but she wanted to take care of it today. She had to go to the paper goods store to buy all the plates, cups, napkins, plastic cutlery, and serving pieces. Then she wanted to go to the bakery and order a picture cake, where they would imprint an actually photo of the kids onto the cake. She didn't have to worry about the rest of the food, because they had a hired a caterer to make all the breakfast-type foods: pancakes, eggs, waffles, bagels, and hash browns.

After a tiring outing, Lori made it back home still in one piece. It was interesting watching the way the kids interacted on their trip. Emma seemed to love getting pushed around in the stroller, observing all the crowds, smiling and waving to passersby. Matthew, on the other hand, covered his face with his hands whenever someone said hello. Lori got lots of comments on how adorable the twins were, and that always made her feel proud.

Lori took the kids out of their car seats. She put Emma down and let her walk to the door, but she carried Matthew. Emma had started walking, but Matthew seemed to be taking his time. Lori was struck by the fact that the competition between siblings had already begun, and she vowed to never let it affect her kids the way it had affected her life. That is, if she could help it.

The next couple of weeks flew by. Finally, it was the Thursday before the party. Lori's parents were supposed to arrive on Friday, which was nice because they would have that extra time to spend with the kids. All the other relatives were coming on Sunday. Although Hannah had said that she would try to come, when she told Lori it wasn't going to work out, Lori had to admit that she was relieved.

Lori and David bathed the kids together on Thursday night. They were finally getting the hang of this twin thing.

"Do you think we have everything we need for Sunday?" Lori said as she washed Emma's hair.

"Lori, we've been through this twenty times! Don't worry about it. You've outdone yourself. It'll be a spectacular party." David was drying Matthew off with a towel.

"I'm so nervous."

"Just relax!"

David and Lori carried the kids out the bathtub. Emma was crying and saying, "More!" Matthew looked relieved to be done.

Just then, the phone rang. David said, "You go get it. I'll finish getting the kids ready for bed."

Lori walked into her bedroom, the closest room with a phone. She glanced at the caller ID, and when she saw her parents' number, her heart sank.

She picked up the receiver. "Hello?"

"Hi, Lori. It's Mom."

"How are you doing? We're all getting excited for tomorrow." Lori tried to sound cheerful.

"Umm...that's why I'm calling. You know how badly Dad and I want to be at the birthday party."

Lori knew what was coming next. No, she didn't know how badly they wanted to be there! "Great. So I'm so happy you'll be coming," she said, trying to play dumb.

"It's not going to work out. We'll have to cancel and take a rain check."

Lori felt devastated. "How can you take a rain check? We can't switch the date of the party!" Her voice cracked; she tried not to let on that she was about to cry. "Why can't you come?" Lori was sure she knew why before she even asked.

"I'm terribly sorry. Believe me, we were really looking

forward to this trip. It's just that Hannah isn't feeling well, and she called us and asked if we can come help her. I'm really sorry." Elaine sounded like she meant it.

But Lori was fuming. Controlling her fury, she said, "Enjoy your time with Hannah."

"I'm sorry, Lori. Send my love to the kids and David. Hopefully, we'll come for a visit when Hannah is feeling better."

Lori hung up the phone and began to sob. It was just too much. Who did Hannah think she was? She had done this to Lori so many times in her life. And what did her parents think they were doing? Just because Hannah said she wasn't feeling well, they were going drop everything, cancel their plans, and run to take care of her? Lori was mad and sad and totally mixed up.

"Lori, I need your help," David was calling from the twins' room.

But Lori just lay face down on the bed, crying.

David came into the room. "Lori? Lori! What's wrong?"

"It's Mom and Dad...they canceled their trip... Hannah's not feeling well...so they are going to...visit her instead," Lori said between sobs.

"I'll call them right now. I'm sure they don't realize how much this means to you!" David sounded hurt, too, which was unusual.

"No, there's no point." Lori was calming down.

"I'm just going to try."

"No. Thanks, but I don't want you to." Lori blew her nose, got control of herself, and stood up. "Where are the kids?"

"They're in their cribs."

"Did you read them a book?"

"Not yet."

"I'll go read to them tonight."

Lori stopped talking.

"So how was the party?"

"It was fun. Except for the fact that I was in a bad mood and couldn't stop thinking about how mad I felt. Everyone asked where my parents were. That didn't help matters and made me more embarrassed. Other than that, all the guests had a great time. Emma and Matthew looked adorable. The cake came out cute."

"Well, that sounds really painful. Did Hannah ever acknowledge that she felt bad about causing your parents to miss the party?"

"No. Although if she had, it would probably have made me angrier. She has this way of saying things that would almost surely turn an apology into an insult."

"Well, you seem like one strong and successful woman to me. So all I can say is that you must have found some inner strength to overcome these very painful experiences. I don't think I would have come through like you."

Lori contemplated what Dr. Wilson had just said. She appreciated those words and felt comfort in his understanding and appreciation for all that she'd experienced.

"Well, our session is over for today. Looking forward to the next one."

"Thank you, once again. And if you remember, I'd love to see pictures of your boys." Lori got up slowly. She had to head back to reality. Time to continue working on all the trip preparations.

CHAPTER 17

ORI OPENED THE DOOR TO Dr. Wilson's office. He was sitting, with something in his hand.

"You remembered the picture!" Lori couldn't keep the surprise out of her voice.

"Of course!"

"So let me see." Now Lori was curious. *Why would Ron not keep any pictures on display in his office, but be almost eager to show this to me today?*

Dr. Wilson handed the picture to her. There were three boys sitting on the front steps of a house. They must have been around thirteen, ten, and eight. The oldest boy had red curly hair, was skinny, and had glasses. The next boy had auburn hair. The youngest boy had red hair, too, but it wasn't as bright as that of the oldest boy.

"The middle boy looks the most like you," Lori commented.

"Yes, that's what people tell me. And his personality is the most similar to mine, too."

"Does that impact your relationship with him?" Lori was pushing it and she knew it.

"It's a challenging job, Lori, to treat your kids in a way that they don't feel that one is more loved than the other. Obviously, you've experienced that in your personal life. But I assure you that you are not alone in your grievances. Research has consistently shown that the biggest grievance adults have toward their parents is perceived favoritism. Even people in their later years, meaning in their eighties, will still recall vividly how a sibling was 'more loved' than them. I should add that research has also shown that those perceptions are oftentimes inaccurate."

"I know that I have my own grievances. But now I'm trying not to perpetuate this issue into my own children's lives. And I'm afraid that I'm messing up."

"What exactly do you mean?"

It was a Sunday morning, and David was in the mood to make blueberry pancakes for everyone. He needed blueberries, though.

"Lori!" he called up the stairs.

"What?"

"I'm running to the grocery store. I want to pick up some blue-berries to make pancakes."

"Fine. Can you also get some milk? We are totally out of milk."

David grabbed his keys and headed out the door. It was pretty early for a Sunday morning, so the store should be relatively quiet. David liked shopping this way best.

As he began pushing the cart into the store, he glimpsed Emma and Matthew's pre-K teacher, Ms. Sarah, a little farther up ahead. She was picking out some apples. She looked up as he passed, so he gave her a big smile and a nice wave. She smiled back, but then pushed her cart in his direction. It looked like she was head-ed toward him.

"David, I'm so happy I bumped into you. I've been meaning to call you."

"What's up?" David couldn't help wondering if there was some sort of problem. Was Matthew acting aggressively? Was Emma not listening?

"Well, do you mind if we talk here?"

"Sure. What's on your mind?" Now David was getting nervous.

"I tried to talk to Lori about this a couple of times, but she totally blew me off. I'm not sure what the problem is, but I figured I would talk to you about it and maybe you'll have an idea."

"Try me." Now David's curiosity was piqued.

"Emma is doing great," Ms. Sarah began. "She's a bright girl. She's sociable. She has lots of friends. She's totally appropriate for our classroom."

"But there's a problem with Matthew?"

"I don't know if you would call it a problem… Matthew is a genius. Literally. Vivian and I have been teaching for many years and neither of us recalls having had a kid like him. He's reading chapter books, writing paragraphs, and doing fifth- or sixth-grade math problems. We've never seen anything like it."

"Yeah, we know he's really smart. There's a history in the family," David said nonchalantly.

"No, let me be clear. He needs to be in a school for gifted kids. A regular school will not be an appropriate environment for him. He needs social interaction with other kids who are similar to him, and he needs the challenges that only such a school can provide."

"And you said you explained all this to Lori?" David breathed deeply.

"Yes. It was the strangest thing. She wasn't interested in hearing what I had to say. I don't get it. She's an intelligent woman. She's usually so aware of the kids' needs. She basically told Vivian and me that under no circumstances would she put Matthew in a special school. Did she discuss it with you?"

"Not really." The answer was not at all, but David felt foolish answering that way.

"Well, maybe you guys can discuss it further or meet with some psych-ed person who can give you direction. Whatever the case, something has to be done."

"Thanks for sharing this information." David tried to smile.

"I hope it wasn't weird to go behind Lori's back like this," Ms. Sarah said, "but I felt like you had to know, too."

"You made a good decision. We'll see you tomorrow." David hurried off to buy the blueberries and milk.

David slowly pulled into the driveway. He was trying to think of the best way to discuss this with Lori. He was upset that she hadn't shared that valuable information, but he knew he'd have to play it smart when he brought up the topic. Lori could be a stubborn woman, and he didn't want to ruin his chances of getting her to see things differently.

As David entered the house, Emma came running and jumped into his arms. "Hi, Daddy! Mommy said you bought blueberries!"

David gave Emma a big hug. "Yup! We're gonna have Daddy's famous blueberry pancakes for breakfast."

He looked around for Matthew. He was lying on the floor, reading. That was Matthew. Why hadn't David realized on his own that he was going to need a different school? "Hi, Matthew!" David called out, knowing that his son would be too engrossed in his book to reply.

"Hi," Matthew mumbled, without even looking up.

An hour later, everyone was sitting around the kitchen table enjoying delicious blueberry pancakes.

"Lori, I need to speak to you about something."

"What?" Lori was already responding in a defensive manner. She must have detected something in David's tone.

"Can we talk privately after we're all done with breakfast?"

"Stop!" Matthew yelled at Emma, who was apparently jabbing his pancake with her fork.

"Emma!" Lori gave her a stern look. Then she turned her attention back to David. "That's fine with me."

When breakfast was finished, David set the kids up with a Diego movie. Then he sat down with Lori in the kitchen.

"What's up?" Lori questioned David in a not very friendly tone.

David struggled to find the right words. "Well, when I was in the grocery store this morning, I met Ms. Sarah. She said she has an issue with Matthew, and she's tried to talk to you about it a couple of times, but you seemed completely uninterested."

"About putting Matthew in a special school? You're absolutely correct. I'm not interested! I'm not going to do that to Emma. I said that I would never create the situation that I grew up in for my own kids. I won't start it now."

"So you think that this will make life difficult for Emma?" David tried to stay calm. It was his only chance of making headway.

"Yes! She'll become what I was — second best to a child prodigy. I can't bear to see Emma relive what I experienced as a child."

"And what about Matthew? He's your child, too. Are you willing to ruin his life so that Emma can be happy?"

Lori was stumped. Then she got her bearings back. "Being in a regular school will not ruin Matthew's life. Who said that being groomed for genius is good for a kid, anyhow? Look where it got Hannah — into an emotional mess with no stable relationships."

This time, David had no response. "I don't know. But I stand my ground. I still think this is a bad decision for Matthew. And if it's bad for Matthew, it'll end up hurting Emma, too. Even if we don't switch Matthew's school, we have to take his talents seriously and give him room to develop in the areas he's good at. Just be careful that you aren't allowing your past to warp your ability to make good decisions."

"And how exactly do you expect me to do that? Everybody's past comes into play when they make decisions. And sometimes, past experiences are valuable sources of information." Lori's voice was getting louder. "You'll never know what it felt like to be me, growing up as Hannah's younger sister. I think it's good that I can use those experiences to change the way I raise our own kids."

"Lori, I think you need therapy!" David made that comment in frustration, but wished he could take it back the minute it left his lips.

"I'm not interested in discussing this anymore." Lori had lowered her voice, but it now had a stony edge to it.

David and Lori cleaned up the kitchen in silence.

"So how did you resolve the issue?" Dr. Wilson asked.

"We haven't, even though this happened some time ago. David has been giving me all this research to support the view that Matthew needs a different school, but I've been trying to ignore it."

"What do you mean, 'trying'?"

"I've been ignoring it when I talk to him, but it's been consuming my thoughts throughout the day."

"What exactly do you think about?"

"Maybe, in my desire to not let Matthew's genius destroy Emma's life, I'm making Emma's needs destroy Matthew's life. It's just too confusing for me. Do I really have to pick one kid over the other? I don't understand how parents make the right decisions."

"You can't come up with a way that both kids can get what they need?"

Lori shuffled her legs as she thought. "I guess I can help Emma develop her own talents — and make sure she feels that those talents are important in their own right." With a sigh, she added, "I think it would have been easier if I'd only had one child."

"Oh, come on, Lori. Despite all the sibling rivalry and difficult relationships, people who grow up with siblings have less chances of developing psychological disorders as adults. For some reason, being forced to deal with these intense emotional relationships as a kid helps a person develop the strength one needs for life." Dr. Wilson looked at her. "Like what happened to you."

Lori thought some more. "I feel so insecure in my ability to make objective decisions for the twins."

"Well, David sounds like a great guy to discuss things with. Remember, decisions about your kids are joint decisions. And you're lucky to have such a nice, healthy person to make the decisions with." Dr. Wilson went out on a limb with that one. He didn't really know that David was an emotionally healthy person. But based on the pieces of information that Lori had shared, he had a strong suspicion that he was correct in his assumption.

Lori blushed. Was Dr. Wilson admonishing her for taking too much control when it came to decision-making in her house?

She glanced down at her watch. Oh my goodness. The session was almost over. She hadn't planned on talking about this at all.

"You know, I just want to add something." Dr. Wilson looked slightly uncomfortable. "I am, in no way, an expert at decision-making for kids' lives. Believe me, I struggle with many decisions myself. I'm always second-guessing what I do. But I try my best, just as you are doing. You are a dedicated mother, Lori, and your kids are lucky to have you. I know you take all decisions seriously, wanting the best for your kids' emotional well-being, and that's a lot more than many people do. I know you'll work this through."

Lori felt better when she heard Dr. Wilson's words. It was true. She was lucky to have David to make decisions with. And she was trying her best.

She stood up. "This session played out differently than I thought it would, but I'm happy we had this discussion. See you next time."

"Lori, you should know that you always give me things to think about, too."

CHAPTER 18

"Hi, David." Lori was talking on her cell phone as she walked across the parking lot. "How's your headache?"

"Thanks for asking. I took some Motrin and it feels a lot better."

"Listen, do you mind putting some dinner up? I know I said I would be coming home early tonight and could take care of dinner, but I just got a call about a meeting that I'm needed for at the clinic. I'll have to stop there after my appointment with Dr. Wilson, which is in five minutes. I won't get home until six thirty."

"No problem. Do you need me to take care of any trip-related items?"

"Hmmm... I can't think of anything right now. Thanks, though." Lori walked into the building and pushed the up button for the elevator.

"How was clinic today?"

"Fine. What about your day?" Lori continued talking as she waited for the elevator to arrive. She felt slightly giddy, almost like she was dating David again.

"I did a great activity with my eleventh graders, but I'll tell you about it when you get home."

"Thanks for everything, David." Lori wasn't sure why she added that, but she suddenly meant it.

"Love you, Lori."

"Love you." Lori hung up the phone and smiled. She'd had a better week with David, that was for sure. Something was working.

She opened the door to Dr. Wilson's office and glanced down at her watch. Right on time. She had not been late for one appointment. Just as she sat down and picked up a magazine, Dr. Wilson poked his head out of his office and said, "Come on in, Lori," with a big smile.

Lori walked in and sat in the chair on the side of the room across from where she normally sat. Not for any particular reason other than the fact that she felt like shaking things up a little.

"Well, how is everything going?"

"I'm doing well, actually, in one noticeable way. I've been arguing much less frequently with David."

"That's great to hear!"

Lori nodded her head slowly and then added, "I was wondering if I could talk about a dream I had a few nights ago? It's really bothering me."

Dr. Wilson said, "By all means. Go ahead."

"Okay, so I'm sitting on this bus. I don't recognize anyone, but the bus is full of people: men, women, and children. The bus is pretty old. The seats are ripped; the walls have graffiti painted on them. It's daytime, but pretty gray looking outside the windows. Suddenly, I have an impending sense of doom. I want to warn everyone, but I don't even know where the danger is coming from.

"Then the bus starts lurching. We're driving off the road! Screams fill the air, and we can see debris flying everywhere. People on the bus are running to the doors, even as the bus keeps moving. Then the bus jerks to a stop. The doors open and we all pour out. I'm screaming that we need to get out of there. Everyone is running.

"Suddenly, I notice strange, sharp wires poking out of the

ground. As people run past, it rips the skin off their bodies. Oddly, they don't seem to notice. They continue running, but as I look at the people, I realize that they're now running skeletons. I see a girl exiting the bus. She's about to walk by a wire. I scream 'No!' and then run to protect her. As I come near, she screams in horror. I look down and realize that I, myself, am a skeleton."

"Wow. That's a pretty powerful dream."

Lori nodded.

"So what are your thoughts about it?"

"Well, I guess its meaning is pretty obvious to me. The skeletons are my clients with anorexia. I want to help them, but then I realize that I'm in the same predicament as them. I myself need help, so how can I help them?"

"That's an interesting interpretation, but I don't understand it. You always seem confident about your work. Your clinic is successful. You have so many success stories. Do you really feel that it's all a scam?"

"No, no, no," Lori answered immediately. "I'm confident in our clinic's methods. And I do feel like I've helped numerous clients recover. But during the summer, I messed up with a client. Actually, it was with the client's mother. My past issues came back to haunt me, and I erred in a conversation with her. The mother then pulled her daughter out of our program at a very precarious stage.

"It haunts me every night. I'm pretty certain that this girl won't make it. And if only I could've taken back that conversation, I bet the girl would have stayed at our clinic and would be recovering today…"

"Do you want to tell me about the conversation you had with her mother?"

"Thanks." Lori wasn't sure how to say what she was thinking.

"It's hard for me to bring this up. I feel so vulnerable admitting my error as a therapist."

"We all make mistakes, Lori. We're human and we've chosen a profession with a vast gray area. If we expect to be perfect, we're doomed."

"I know that rationally, but it doesn't make my mistakes easier to live with emotionally. And it certainly does not help my pride."

"I understand."

Lori looked at Dr. Wilson and knew that he meant what he had said.

"Anyway, here's what happened. We had taken in an almost fifteen-year-old girl with severe anorexia. She'd been at our clinic for a month, and had made minimal progress. She was maintaining her weight at eighty-six pounds, which was a dangerously low BMI of 14. She was resistant to therapy and rarely engaged during any of her sessions. As is often the case when a more difficult case presents itself, I was called in to try to help. I began seeing her for an hour session each morning. Even I was making almost no progress. And then suddenly, I had this breakthrough session with her, where she told me about her older brother, who had taken up all her parents' time, energy, and resources.

"To make a long story short, during her description of her childhood, I became tangled up in her story. I felt like I was reliving my childhood. I became enraged at her parents. I tried calming myself down, to remind myself to remain objective, but it was extremely difficult.

"We ended the session with me suggesting that we explore the option of family therapy to talk about these issues that were obviously festering inside her. The girl was not opposed to the idea, so I suggested that I talk to her mother about it. Again, the girl agreed. After she left the room, I gave myself some time to relax and assure myself that I was thinking objectively. Believing that I was totally calm and rational, I went to look for the girl's mother to set up some therapy time, and possibly even suggest that her husband try to fly in for a few sessions, too. But this topic was much more emotional than I was prepared for."

Lori walked rapidly down the hallway. She wasn't sure where to find Katie, Allison's mom, but she did want to find her quickly. She had only a half hour before she had to be at a meeting, and she wanted to come up with a new family therapy plan for Allison. Lori knew that Allison's mom attended one of the parent workshops on Monday mornings. It should be over around now, so Katie could be in the coffee room getting a drink. That was the first place Lori would check.

Sure enough, as Lori pushed the door to the coffee room open, she could see Katie sitting on a chair, sipping a coffee with another mom. As Lori approached her, Katie glanced up.

"Katie, I wanted to talk to you briefly. Do you have some time to come to my office?"

"Sure," Katie answered, but she looked unsure. Her short brown hair framing her face, along with her tightly pulled lips, gave her the look of a stern and difficult woman. Suddenly, Lori was not convinced that this conversation was going to be as simple as she'd imagined.

Katie followed Lori out the door. Walking down the hallway, Lori attempted to make small talk. "How's everything going?" she asked, trying to sound as friendly as possible.

"Pretty good." Katie was still not smiling.

Lori could not help thinking: *Like mother, like daughter.*

"It's often very challenging for the parents to find ways to occupy themselves while their children are here in our program. But it means a lot to have a parent here. So we do our best to offer classes and create programming for parents, too."

Katie just pursed her lips tighter and nodded. Lori found herself suddenly wishing she'd taken the time to develop more of a relationship with Katie before now. It would have made what she had to do now a lot easier.

They continued walking in silence. Somehow, the silence seemed deafening. Finally, they were in front of Lori's office. Lori opened the door and Katie followed her in. Lori motioned for Katie to have a seat, as Lori sat beside her desk. Katie was dressed meticulously. She was wearing a fashionable gray silk blouse with a white pencil skirt. Her makeup was done perfectly; her mauve-colored lipstick outlined her lips in flawless symmetry. She had the look of an overachieving perfectionist.

Lori swallowed hard. She would not allow herself to feel intimidated, even though she was starting to feel a little more nervous than her usual confident self. She thought back to the really sad conversation she'd had with Allison a short while ago. Looking at Katie, she could relate to all that Allison had shared with her. And then Lori felt mad again.

"Well, I met with Allison for her therapy session a short while ago." Lori paused and looked at Allison's mom. Her lips were still pursed, but her eyes looked anxious. Lori was almost happy that Katie seemed nervous. She could not help thinking that Katie should be concerned that Allison finally spilled the beans.

"It was a real breakthrough session," Lori added. Then she

paused again, allowing the suspense to build. She felt like she was being cruel, but she couldn't stop herself.

"Are you going to tell me about it?" Katie said in an even tone.

"As you know, we've been having a difficult time engaging Allison during therapy. All our therapists are struggling to reach her. She seems so far away."

"You are not telling me anything new." Katie was obviously annoyed. Lori was almost enjoying herself.

"I just want you to follow my progression. Anyway, today I brought up a topic, and it was like a wall came crashing down and years of built-up feelings came pouring out. Allison finally told me about Will." Lori looked at Katie to gauge the effects of her words.

Katie breathed in deeply and bit her lip. It was obvious that this was a difficult subject. Lori continued. "Allison told me all about his ODD diagnosis and the years of therapies, drugs, and school programs that you and your husband dedicated your-selves to. This is very honorable on your part, but Allison was sharing with me the extreme difficulties of being Will's younger sister. I think these may be some of the underlying emotional issues that Allison is struggling with. And I think that family therapy would be the best format in which to address this."

As Lori was speaking, Katie was shaking her head back and forth vigorously, and her eyebrows were knitted tightly together. And then she spoke up. "Stop, please! Allison is totally lying. That's not the way it was."

Lori felt the anger boiling inside her. How dare Katie turn this around? Now she wanted to accuse Allison of lying? No wonder Allison was in such a difficult emotional state. But Lori tried to stay calm and professional. "I know it's often hard to hear the 'other side of the story.' I'm sure you have your side, too. That's why I think we really have to set up some family therapy time so you can each express your side, and you can try to mend years of difficult emotional experiences for both of you."

Katie made a noise that sounded pretty close to a snort. "You are so wrong. This is Allison's issue. Not mine. You're missing the point."

Now Lori was losing it. "Can you stop a minute and just try to think like Allison? Just for one minute? She's dying, unless we can work together to help her. Just humble yourself for once, and admit that you may have something to do with this!"

Katie stared at Lori, obviously appalled. "You don't know what you're saying, and you're not even giving me a chance to explain things!"

Lori was trying so hard to keep herself composed. "Look, I understand that you've been through torturous times with Will and now with Allison. Accepting that some of Allison's issues have to do with your parenting style through those trying times does not mean you're a bad parent. Accepting this, and then being willing to work on it, will make you that much of a better parent, that much of a better person..."

Lori was going way too quickly in this conversation, and she knew it was doomed. She also knew that she was going against current research and political correctness by putting blame on the parents. She had no right to go there. But she couldn't stop herself. She just kept imagining it was her own mother sitting in front of her, her own mother refusing to acknowledge that she had made mistakes by ignoring Lori's issues, in order to deal with Hannah's. Her own mother saying that Lori was lying about her past!

Katie's face was flushed. "Oh, now you're blaming this whole anorexia thing on me? Are you out of your mind? You're not listening to a thing I'm trying to say! You call yourself a therapist?!"

Suddenly, Lori had had it. Her voice was louder than she wanted it to be. "Yes, I'm blaming it on you! Until you accept some responsibility, your daughter will not get better. She needs you to tell her that you made mistakes. She's dying for your attention — literally. When will you wake up?"

Katie's eyes were flaming. "Not only are you a disgrace, this whole clinic is a scam! My daughter has been here for over a month and you've done nothing for her. You've charged us thousands of dollars, and all you can come up with is that this whole thing is my fault? I'm taking Allison out right now." Katie stood up and folded her arms together. "And what's more, you'll be hearing from my lawyer." Then Katie turned around and stormed out the door.

Lori had messed up. Badly. She had no right to blame Katie. It was cruel, unprofessional, and probably incorrect.

Lori looked at Dr. Wilson. "And that was it. She pulled her daughter out. We never heard from her lawyer, but I won't be surprised if we do at some point in the future."

"That was a powerful story. But I'm not sure what the crux of the issue is. Which part is bothering you the most? That you blamed Katie? You probably shouldn't have gone there, but there was some truth to what you said. The fact that Katie reacted so strongly makes it more likely that there were seeds of reality in it." Dr. Wilson was looking at her intently.

"I've played and replayed that conversation in my head. There's something I'm missing. I was too emotionally involved, and I feel like I jumped to conclusions. If I could have stayed calm, taken the conversation slower, not have imagined my mother sitting in front of me, I could have easily set up the family therapy time, and Katie would not have taken Allison out of our clinic. I could've expressed the same ideas in a totally different format, and Katie would've been fine with what I said."

"I'm not so sure, Lori. I agree that you're connecting to Allison in an emotionally and professionally unhealthy way. But I don't think you can blame yourself for any of this. There were obviously deep family issues that were not going to be fixed easily, no matter how much therapy you gave them. Even if they stayed, you had a steep battle to fight."

Lori leaned back in her seat and closed her eyes. "I guess that's my real issue. I can't get past this. I've spent hours online scanning obituaries from the city that Allison lives in. I'm so scared she died, and I can't stop blaming myself."

"It's tough," Dr. Wilson said. "Believe me, I know. I've had two patients commit suicide over the years, and it haunts me to this day. I sometimes wonder if I could have done things differently..."

"Yeah, Ron, I know. I chose a profession that has this risk involved. It's just not fun."

"Especially in the field of eating disorders. I don't have to tell you that anorexia has the highest fatality rate of all psychiatric disorders."

"I know, I know. But I don't want anyone to die! Death is too final for me. It just doesn't feel fair."

"Now you're getting into deep philosophical issues. What is death and dying? Why is it so hard for us to accept it? Is death really the end?"

"Are you scared of dying?" Lori's pleading eyes wanted comfort.

"I've gone through times in my life when I've been more or less scared. It's the reality we're all heading to. We can't escape it, just avoid it for a while. Are you scared of dying?"

"Isn't it obvious?" Lori replied. "Yes, I'm scared. But I know that the more I self-actualize, the more my fears diminish. I've learned to control my fears over the years."

The room was quiet. Lori and Dr. Wilson were contemplating everything they had discussed.

Finally, Dr. Wilson gave a cough, moved forward in his seat, and put his hands on his knees. "Well, time is up."

"Thanks for letting me get that off my chest. I'll see you next session." Lori stood up more slowly than usual. Her thoughts were in overdrive again. Even after that whole discussion, she wondered where Allison was now. She wondered if she was still alive. And then she wondered what it felt like to be dead.

She walked out of the office, still wondering until her mind felt like it would explode. She got into the car and turned the radio on loud to block out all her swirling thoughts as she drove home.

CHAPTER 19

Lori wasn't sure what she wanted to talk about at therapy today. She didn't know why, but her mind felt blank. Maybe she had exhausted all topics and was ready to stop therapy. No way. She had a lot further to go. She entered the office and sat down in her usual spot.

"Hi, Lori. How are you doing?"

"I'm doing well. You know, I was just thinking, as I took the elevator upstairs, that I don't really have anything in particular that I'd like to talk about."

"Hmmm." Dr. Wilson moved back in his chair. "In that case, I have an idea."

"What's that?" Lori was hesitant.

"Since we talked about your dream last week, I'm in a dream mode. I'm not a big dream interpreter, but I often have my clients recount any recurring dreams that they may have. Sometimes this gives very telling information. If you feel comfortable, how about sharing a recurring dream of yours?"

Lori knitted her brows and thought fervently. After a couple of minutes, she said, "There's this dream that I often have, but I can't imagine it'll give you any useful information. It's pretty boring. Basic perfectionist dream."

"Try me."

My heart is racing. I'm a junior in college. The semester is over in one week. I have no notes to study for my finals. I haven't completed any of my papers, and I lost the assignment requirements. I'm wandering around my dorm, looking for friends who have notes I can photocopy. But everyone I ask shows me notebooks and notebooks of notes. I can't do it in time. It's impossible.

I'm in a state of frenzy. Would the teachers give me extra time? Maybe they wouldn't notice that I haven't done my papers. Would I fail?

I look up. My chemistry teacher is heading toward me.

"Lori, I'm missing your last assignment."

"I know. I'm almost done. I'll get it to you tomorrow."

How am I going to do what I said? I'm going to fail. Would the college give me an extra chance?

"So what does that tell you?" Lori asked.

Dr. Wilson sat quietly, contemplating. Lori felt the suspense building. Finally, he spoke. "If it's okay with you, can we play this out a little?"

Lori raised her eyebrows. "Sure."

"Then I'd like to backtrack. Can we analyze why you came to see me for therapy at the very beginning?"

Lori looked startled. Dr. Wilson was up to something, but Lori wasn't sure what it was. And she did not like this new role he seemed to be taking, playing a more assertive part. "Isn't it obvious? I have all these pent-up resentments against my parents and Hannah that I wanted to work through."

"I have a different thought. Do you mind if I interject my opinion?"

"Not at all!" Lori answered too quickly, making it pretty obvious that Dr. Wilson's opinion was actually the last thing she wanted to hear right now.

Dr. Wilson either did not notice, or persisted despite this. "I don't think the underlying emotion causing you all this unsettlement is resentment or jealousy."

"You don't?" Lori felt a mixture of curiosity and annoyance.

"No, I don't. I think the resentment is actually a defense." Dr. Wilson seemed sincere in his desire to express his perceptions.

"Can you explain?" Lori knitted her brow, trying to guess where Dr. Wilson was going with this.

"I think the underlying emotion causing you all this unsettlement...is guilt."

"Guilt?" Lori asked, skeptical.

"Yes, guilt. Guilt that you've been so successful in life, when it was always Hannah who was supposed to be so successful. Guilt that you have a husband and kids, that you have a successful job, that you turned out to be so smart, that you have a good life — while Hannah lives alone, is emotionally unstable, and is so sad.

And I think you have to use the resentment to convince yourself that your life is really horrible — that way, you can eliminate the guilt. Because if your life is so bad, you can't feel guilty that Hannah's life isn't working out that great. You are constantly reliving the painful memories of your past so that you can eliminate the guilt you feel for having such a great life."

Lori's head was spinning. She blinked a couple of times. Was Dr. Wilson right?

"It's always interesting when someone shares their past to note the memories that she or he chooses to recall. You have come to me because I'm an expert at psychoanalysis, about understanding people's recollection of their past. So I know very well how a person can create a past by choosing memories to include and memories to leave out. All the memories that you shared with me basically proved what you were trying to convince me: that your parents were more dedicated to Hannah than to you, and that it was hard to be the younger sister to such a prodigy. These factors have had an everlasting impact on your emotional well-being.

"But what about the memories that you didn't share with me? Isn't it interesting that those wonderful ski trips that you once mentioned in passing — during which you had time to connect with your dad, doing something that Hannah didn't enjoy — were not included in the memories that you gave me? I'm sure there are many more memories like that one. Here's another example: Did you make the twins a two-year-old birthday party that your parents did attend?

"As a matter of fact, I'll be so bold as to say that I think that you came to me for therapy, not to overcome the resentment, but to reaffirm these resentments — because for some reason you've felt a surge in guilt recently."

Lori breathed in deeply. She felt angry. Angry that Dr. Wilson had not kept his word. Hadn't he promised that all he would do was listen? She didn't want his opinions! And what right did he have to understand her better than she understood herself? She'd spent years analyzing her actions. Who did he think he was, just jumping in and turning things over?

Then she felt embarrassed. Why hadn't she realized what she was doing? She felt like an idiot. She was a therapist. Why hadn't she come to these conclusions herself? And how did Dr. Wilson know that she had made a huge party for the twins' second birthday, which her parents had attended? In fact, they'd actually stayed for a week, taking the kids on outings every day.

Dr. Wilson just sat there quietly. He seemed to know that Lori needed time to process what he had told her. Doing something like this had the chance to backfire. Lori might just storm out in a huff. But he must have felt that it was worth the risk.

"Lori, the recurring dream you shared with me is common for someone who is successful but never expected to be successful, who feels like he or she is faking the world."

Lori uncrossed her legs and shuffled in her seat. She picked up her water bottle and took a sip.

"Listen to me," Dr. Wilson said. "What happens when you do something fun? What happens when things are going really well in life? How do you feel?"

Lori closed her eyes. "Sad. Worried. Anxious."

"Do you think that's typical?"

"No. I guess you're onto something. I can't ever just enjoy myself, or I'm overcome with guilt."

"Don't you see? One of the worst implications of growing up as Hannah's younger sister was that you envisioned a life for yourself of being second-best. But you're not! And now you don't know how to make sense of it, so you're besieged by guilt."

"I understand your theory. However, there's one problem with it."

Dr. Wilson gave Lori a piercing look, as if he thought she was trying to rationalize her way out of what he said.

"The tipping point on the scale that caused me to come to you was not because something bad happened to Hannah. It was because something really good finally happened to her."

One Month Earlier

When the sound of a ringing phone jolted her awake at

4:47 a.m., Lori knew that something terrible had happened. Trembling, she groped about. With David snoring loudly beside her, and still half-asleep herself, she muttered a tense hello into the receiver.

"Hi, Lori! It's Mom!" Lori's mom sounded giddy with joy.

"And Dad — I'm on the other phone!" Lori could hear the smile in her dad's voice.

"Sorry if we woke you, but we have some really exciting news. We didn't want you to read it in the newspapers before we got a chance to tell you personally."

"Yes?" Lori was still half-asleep. She rubbed her eyes, trying to figure out what could be so exciting in the middle of the night.

"Hannah got a phone call from Stockholm about a half hour ago. She's won the Nobel Prize in Physics, together with John Kirby, the professor she did her fellowship with at MIT! It had to do with a theory she developed while she was at MIT relating to the conservation of water, freezing water atoms, analyzing water atoms from years ago, as well as its impact on global warming and the possibilities for decreasing drought in the world."

"Congratulations! That's fantastic!" Lori was too tired to think coherently.

"Hey, Lori, you're the sister of a Nobel laureate! What do you say to that?" Lori's dad let out a laugh. "Unbelievable, huh?"

"Thanks for calling. I'll call you back in the morning when I can think more clearly."

"Talk to you tomorrow then," Lori's mom said. "And one more thing. Block off the week of December 10 on your calendar. We're all going to Sweden for the Nobel Prize ceremonies!"

David rolled over. Having heard the congratulations, he asked who had a baby.

"No, no, no. It's not that at all. Much bigger news."

And then, for the second surprise that night, Lori found herself sobbing.

David suddenly sat up straight. "What's going on?"

Lori slowly calmed down. "Hannah won the Nobel Prize in Physics. It'll be in the newspapers tomorrow morning."

David's jaw dropped. "That's wonderful! She's dedicated her life to helping mankind, and now the world has recognized it. But why are you crying?"

Lori blew her nose. "I don't know. I'm happy for her. I really am. But Mom and Dad are expecting us to come to the Nobel Prize ceremonies."

"Lori, that's phenomenal! That's a chance of a lifetime. I mean a chance in a million. Who gets to go to the Nobel Prize ceremonies? It's supposed to be amazing. The king and queen of Sweden are there. There's a huge banquet. I've read a lot about it." Now David seemed giddy.

"I don't think I want to go."

"What are you saying?"

"I don't know. It's just too much. My relationship with Hannah and my parents — I don't think I can handle it."

"But you'll regret this forever if you miss it!"

"No, maybe you will regret it forever."

"Come on, Lori. Maybe it's time you finally got yourself in therapy and dealt with all these feelings you've bottled inside you all these years."

"David, I hate when you say that!" she started crying again.

"Fine, I take it back. I'm sorry. Let's go back to bed and talk again in the morning, when we're more awake." David lay back down. "Just curious. Why did they have to call in the middle of the night?"

Lori's eyes were already closed. "It's morning in Sweden. They call when they announce it there."

The phone rang nonstop the next morning. Aunts, uncles, and cousins were all calling to share in the exciting news. It was madhouse getting the kids off to school and getting ready for work. Lori tried calling Hannah, but couldn't get through. David tried explaining to Emma and Matthew that Aunt Hannah had won a really big prize for her discovery in science.

It wasn't until Lori was on lunch break at the clinic that she finally had time to process the events of the last hours. David's words about seeking therapy kept replaying in her head.

"And that's when I picked up the phone and made an appointment with you," Lori concluded.

Dr. Wilson sat there in amazement. It was his turn to be speechless. Finally, he said, "Hannah won the Nobel Prize?"

"Yes, and we're leaving to Sweden to attend the ceremonies in less than two weeks." Lori waited and then continued, "So now, how does this fit with your theory?"

"I'm still convinced that what I said has truth to it." Dr. Wilson clasped his hands together and looked at the ceiling. "Let's talk about it some more next time."

"But next time will be the last session I can get in before we leave to Sweden. I need help dealing with the trip."

"I'll try, Lori, but you are not expecting easy answers."

"Yeah, I know."

CHAPTER 20

A S LORI DROVE TO DR. Wilson's office, her mind was on the Nobel Prize ceremonies. The suitcases were packed, as they were leaving to Stockholm in two days. Lori was apprehensive, but it was mostly normal nerves — like hoping the plane ride would be smooth, Emma and Matthew would act appropriately throughout the ceremonies and dinners, the clothes Lori was bringing would be appropriate for the different events, and so on. The knot that Lori had had in her stomach that ached when she thought about attending a ceremony to celebrate Hannah's achievements had slowly dissipated. Lori wasn't sure if this was due to Dr. Wilson's insights, or to the burden-lifting experience of having someone finally understand what she had been through in her life.

Lori was happy that she had managed to schedule this last appointment before she left. She just needed a little more confidence and guidance. And she wanted to finish understanding Dr. Wilson's theory.

Her mind continued to process the way this event was impacting the people around her. Elaine and Sam seemed happier than they had been in years. They were calling Lori every few hours to remind her about different things she had to bring. In the last phone call, they had suggested that she rehearse some comments with Emma and Matthew in case they were interviewed. They also mentioned that the winner of the Nobel Prize in Chemistry was bringing his two sons, who were eleven and thirteen, and one of the winners of the Nobel Prize in Physiology was bringing three grandchildren ranging from ages four to ten. Lori was relieved to know that Emma and Matthew would not be the only children in attendance.

David was giddy with excitement. He thought it was going to be an intriguing experience to be in the presence of all the different celebrities and to attend all the dinners and banquets. Lori had never guessed that this would be something that David would enjoy so much.

Emma and Matthew were excited, too. Emma was mostly looking forward to seeing the king and queen of Sweden, while Matthew was looking forward to hearing the Stockholm Philharmonic Orchestra, as he had recently developed an interest in orchestras.

Lori had spoken to Hannah earlier in the day. Hannah sounded content in a way that Lori had never heard her sound before. Most surprising, in an un-Hannah-like conversation, she thanked Lori profusely for arranging to come to the ceremonies and for bringing the whole family. Hannah said that it touched her deeply. Lori responded that she wouldn't have missed this for the world. It wasn't a lie. After many sessions of therapy, she meant this sincerely.

Lori turned left onto the street where Dr. Wilson's office was located. Her thoughts continued to ramble, and she drove as though on autopilot. She had thought about Dr. Wilson's ideas often since the last session's mind-opening experience. Therapy had helped her in ways she could never have imagined.

Before seeing Dr. Wilson, she'd been convinced that she'd analyzed every detail of her life and understood all her actions, and she hadn't been sure how Dr. Wilson was going to help her. Originally, she had thought that she'd benefit from being forced to express bottled-up emotions, but not necessarily from anything that Dr. Wilson could say to her. However, Dr. Wilson had pinpointed and articulated aspects of her thought processes that she had not been aware of. She'd spent the past couple of nights lying awake, wondering if just the knowledge that she had gained would change her interactions, or if she'd have to consciously take the information and convert it to a practical level.

Lori pulled her car into the parking lot. She found a spot right near the entrance to the building. As she got out of the car, she realized she was feeling more satisfied with her life than she had in many years.

"Hi, Lori." Dr. Wilson gave her a warm smile.

"Hi." Lori slowly sat down.

"So, you are leaving tomorrow?"

"Actually, the day after tomorrow."

Dr. Wilson shook his head back and forth. "I can't wait to hear about your trip. Bring back pictures."

"I'm sure we'll have loads."

"How are you feeling about the whole trip? Any better?"

"Yes. Much better, actually. I'm trying to understand why." Lori stopped and then quickly added, "And you wouldn't believe this, but Hannah called to tell me how much it means to her that I'm coming with the whole family."

"That must feel great." Dr. Wilson looked at her intently. "So you're not sure why you feel better about attending the ceremony?"

She looked back at him. "Well, I think that over time, your sessions have helped me come to terms with my past. The last session was particularly helpful. I'm still curious how you'll explain the last issue of why the news of the Nobel Prize caused me such emotional upheaval. Despite that last piece of the puzzle, your explanation about the guilt that I'm constantly experiencing and the resentment that I use as a defense has really hit home. I've thought about it often, and I agree with your assessment."

"Really?" Dr. Wilson looked a little proud. Lori didn't mind. He deserved to feel that way.

"Yes." She paused. "So what *is* your explanation for the Nobel Prize causing me so much turmoil?" Lori couldn't control herself from asking.

Dr. Wilson leaned forward slightly. "Here's what I came up with. The Nobel Prize is changing the way you viewed life until now. You based your life on trying to decrease the guilt you felt at being so successful while Hannah was so miserable. But now, Hannah's dreams have really come true. Was all that guilt for nothing? Your brain is in overload. You have a need to justify the resentments, to convince yourself that they are real."

Lori pondered his words. It was hard to process information while sitting in a quiet room with Dr. Wilson staring at her intently. "I see what you're saying," she finally replied.

Dr. Wilson continued. "Listen, what I'm telling you isn't black-and-white science. It's an art. You can analyze these scenarios in various ways. I'm giving you a direction that I think is accurate, but even more important, that I think will help you overcome your inner struggles."

Lori again sat quietly for a few moments, looking at the chair to her right. Finally, she looked back at Dr. Wilson and said, "You've definitely helped give me a more positive view of my life and the people around me."

Dr. Wilson didn't say anything, so Lori added, "You know, over the past couple of days, I thought of a couple of ideas to help me deal with my resentments toward my parents and Hannah."

"I'm impressed with your initiative. What are your ideas?"

"The first idea I had was not too difficult. I sat down one night and made a list of different events and times that my parents really helped me out, did something meaningful for me, or just demonstrated that they cared. When I finished, I had a long and significant list. After everything calms down in a few weeks, I'm going to try to write them a thank-you note for all the wonderful memories. I think this will help me get over some of my negative emotions."

"That sounds great."

"To deal with the resentments I have toward Hannah, I thought of another idea."

"You really took the task of finding a solution seriously," Dr. Wilson commented again. He sounded sincere.

"You'd be the first one to understand that this is an aspect of my personality. For good or for bad, when something needs to be done, I have to act. I can't just sit back and take things slowly." Lori shuffled.

"I agree with you that this has been a theme of your life, especially in your later years. What's your idea?"

"I tried to think of something I could do to help alleviate my guilt. My idea was that if I somehow reached out to Hannah and tried to share my life with her, I'd feel that I was using the good things I have been blessed with to help others, and I wouldn't feel as guilty. Does that make sense?"

"Can you explain that a little more?"

"Like feeling guilty that I have a family and she's alone — if I invite her over, have the kids connect to her, and things like that, I won't feel as guilty." Lori looked at Dr. Wilson hesitantly.

"What you're saying sounds good to me. However, be careful not to go overboard in that area, either. Balance is always the healthiest medium. You don't want to create a situation where you're overextending yourself in your kindness because of your need to eliminate the guilt. That will be setting a new defense in place. Although in some ways this a healthier defense, if you get carried away with it, it can have negative implications, as well."

Lori sighed deeply. "Life is complicated."

"As I said last time, there are no easy answers. I think you're off to a great start. You seem to be in a healthier state, and I think you may actually enjoy your trip. Don't misinterpret my hesitation over your idea. I think that what you said has validity. If you can pull it off with the appropriate balance, you'll definitely find greater satisfaction and calmness in life. And I'm sure you will help Hannah have a more meaningful existence, too." Dr. Wilson had a Diet Coke beside him. He took a sip and then looked out the window.

Suddenly, Lori felt an urge to know more about Dr. Wilson. Did he have siblings? What were his relationships with his parents like? What were his life struggles?

"So how much longer do you think I should come to therapy?"

"Lori, I can't answer that question as well as you."

"Well, I know you've helped me a lot. But I'm not ready to let go yet. I want to see how the trip goes and then take it from there. Maybe we can cut back to once a week now."

"That sounds fine to me."

Lori glanced at her watch. There was still some time left, but she didn't have anything in particular that she felt a need to discuss, although she knew that as soon as she walked out of the office a flood of issues would fill her mind.

She sat quietly a little longer. Then she thought of a question. "Do you have any pieces of final wisdom to impart before I head out on my trip? It's going to be intense family time, so I hope we don't have any blowups."

"All I can say is try to let go and really enjoy the experience. When things get intense, look at the big picture. You've given a lot so that Hannah could get to where she is, whether you meant to or not, so enjoy every moment and celebrate this milestone."

"That's an interesting way to think about it," Lori said as she mulled over Dr. Wilson's point.

"Another thought you may want to remember is that your kids will be watching your every move and will be learning from your interactions. This is an opportune time to teach them how to interact as siblings and as sons and daughters."

Lori laughed. "If I can think like that constantly, I guess I'll be on my best behavior."

There were still a few minutes until their time was officially up, but Lori didn't have anything else to say and had a lot to take care of anyway. "I'm going to head out now, because I have numerous errands I still have to run. Thanks for all your help. I hope I can make use of it on the trip."

Dr. Wilson closed his notes. "Have a fantastic trip! I'll be anxiously awaiting your return so I can hear all about it."

Lori stood up. "Have a good couple of weeks." Then she walked out of the office and closed the door behind her.

CHAPTER 21

LORI COULD NOT BELIEVE SHE was back in America and her trip was over. The trip, along with all its implications, had consumed her for the past couple of months. And now it was a memory. An extraordinary memory at that! The whole family was all exhausted, but it worked out well that they returned at the start of winter break. David and the kids were off from school and could catch up on all the sleep they had missed.

Lori entered Dr. Wilson's office, excited to share the events of her time in Sweden. There was so much to talk about.

"Hello!" Dr. Wilson exclaimed as she entered his office, "I can't wait to hear about your trip! I tried to follow any news reports or interviews coming from the Nobel ceremonies. I read a couple of quotes from your kids, and found your family's pictures online in a Swedish paper. I also read about a controversial lecture that Hannah gave."

Lori chuckled. "Yes, it was an unbelievable week." Lori felt good that Dr. Wilson had taken such an interest in the events. "I have so much to share with you. I don't know where to begin."

"So then, as I often say, start at the beginning." Dr. Wilson sat back as though he were looking forward to relishing all the details that Lori was about to share. She couldn't blame him. It had been a fascinating experience. She wondered if the general population realized what went on during that week in Stockholm. With all her preparation, Lori had still not been equipped for the sheer wonderment of it all.

"Well, let's see. We all left on Thursday, December 7. We met my parents and Hannah at JFK Airport, as we were all flying together. I was jittery, but flying with the kids gave me something else to think about."

"Flight 273 to Stockholm now boarding. Flight 273 to Stockholm now boarding."

Lori stood up. "Come on, guys. Time to board the plane."

Matthew started crying.

David looked over at Matthew and asked, "What's wrong?"

"I can't find my book," he said between sobs.

Lori turned to Emma and caught the mischievous gleam in her eyes. "Give it back right now!"

"Lori, how do you know Emma has it?" Lori's mom jumped in.

Lori's dad was bending down and trying to calm Matthew. Hannah was already lining up to board.

"Mom and Dad, can you let David and me handle this?" Lori tried to stay composed; it was going to be a long trip.

Emma sheepishly pulled the book out of her bag.

Matthew grabbed it and gave Emma the dirtiest look he could muster. Lori looked at her mom smugly.

"What? I thought it was my book!" Emma always had an answer or excuse for every mischievous action.

David gave Emma a look, too, but there wasn't time for more than that.

"Let's go, Lori. Hannah's on line already," Lori's mother nudged her impatiently.

Lori began to wonder why she had agreed to this whole trip.

Finally, they all made it onto the plane and settled down. Working out the seating turned into an interesting ordeal. When it was finally settled, Emma was sitting between Elaine and David, Matthew was sitting beside Sam in the row behind, and Lori was sitting across from David and beside Hannah in the center row.

As the trip began, Lori's dad gave Matthew some word puzzles and math challenges to complete. Emma was busy talking to Elaine. David fell asleep. Lori tried to make small talk with her sister.

"This is truly amazing, Hannah."

"Yeah. It's hard to believe I'm on a plane headed toward the Nobel Prize. I feel like I'm going to wake up any moment now, and all this will have been a dream."

"Are you nervous about any parts of the trip?"

"There are two parts that I'm most anxious for. The first one is the acceptance speech I have to give during the banquet in front of at least a thousand celebrities, including new and old Nobel laureates and the Swedish royal family. I've heard that it's almost as if the Nobel committee makes you earn the prize all over again when you give this speech "

"Wow! I can't imagine doing that."

Hannah chuckled. "And you know me. I'm not the best public speaker. I've been practicing my speech almost twenty-four seven for the past week."

"What's the second thing you're nervous about?"

"If you remember, I don't have the best relationship with John Kirby, the professor I'm sharing the prize with. I hope we can act civilly and interact positively throughout the ceremonies."

Hannah reached into her bag as she was talking and pulled out some note cards.

"Is that your speech?"

"Yeah."

"If you want to practice with me, I'd be happy to listen."

"Thanks. I'll read it to myself a few more times, and then I think I will take you up on your offer." Hannah gave Lori a grateful look.

Lori felt good. She turned to look at everyone else. Everything seemed calm, so she put her head back and let herself doze off for a little while.

An hour later, Lori opened her eyes. She looked around. Hannah had dozed off, too, her note cards on her lap. She looked over toward her dad and Matthew. Matthew looked engrossed in whatever he was doing. Sam noticed her looking at them. "Lori," he said, "Matthew is astounding! I have him doing algebra problems, and he's breezing through them. Are you aware of his abilities? We have another genius on our hands. I knew he was good, but I didn't realize just how good."

Lori's mind felt completely muddled. At first, she felt a surge of pride. Her dad was connecting to her kid in the way she had always dreamed he would connect to her. She felt like saying to Hannah, "Now look at that!" It seemed so immature, but she felt as though she had finally won. And then, at the next moment, she felt a terrible surge of guilt. She automatically glanced toward Emma to see if she was listening. It wasn't fair. Look at the way Sam valued math genius. It seemed that that was the only way he could value a kid. Lori never wanted Emma to experience the pain of being second best because she was not a math genius.

"Lori, you didn't answer." The excitement was evident on Sam's face. "We have another budding Nobel Prize winner. What are you doing for him?"

Lori bit her lip. If they were alone, she may have lashed out and all her resentments would have come pouring out. But they were on a crowded plane, so she restrained herself and thought before answering. It was better this way because when she finally expressed herself, she said something she'd always wanted to say, but in a controlled way.

"Dad, David and I know that Matthew has unusual talents. We also know that Emma has wonderful talents, too. We're trying our best to give them whatever they need so that they can develop their unique abilities and also grow to be emotionally healthy adults."

"Oh." Her dad seemed to know that Lori's words had deeper allusions. She glanced over at Hannah and was relieved to see she was still sleeping. She did not intend for Hannah to hear these words. Lori felt a pang of guilt and wondered whether her father understood that she was — unfairly — implicating him in Hannah's emotional struggles.

Sam looked over at Lori. "Lori, you always had a phenomenal talent for understanding human emotions. I guess that's why you've become a true expert in your field. Your kids are lucky that you're their mom. I'm sure you and David are doing a much better job at balancing the twins' needs than Mom and I did at balancing yours and Hannah's. We messed up often. Didn't we?"

Lori had never expected that response. She bit her lip to prevent a surge of tears from cascading out of her eyes. Why did this conversation have to take place on an airplane, with people all around? Her face felt hot and tingly.

She swallowed hard and blew her nose and said, "Oh, Dad, please don't say that. You tried your best, and look at how your two children turned out: a Nobel Prize winner, who's helped the world in ways that will be playing out for years to come, and a best-selling author and world-renowned psychologist, who's a dedicated mother to two possible world changers. This trip is really an honor to you. You should be proud of all that you've done. I know parenting wasn't — and isn't — an easy task."

Suddenly, Lori felt sympathy for her parents in a way she had never felt before. She looked around to make sure no one was listening. It was hard to be sure, but no one seemed to have noticed the intense exchange of words that had just taken place.

Lori's dad pulled out a tissue and blew his nose, too. "Thanks, Lori. I can't tell you how much those words mean to me."

"Grandpa, look! I got this one. Is it correct?" Matthew tugged on Sam's shirt.

Matthew seemed alive in a way that Lori did not normally see him. She knew then that everybody's advice that Matthew needed a new school was accurate.

Lori's dad smiled at her. "Better give him a new one," and he turned back to Matthew.

Lori turned to Emma and her mother once again. She didn't think her mom had overheard their conversation. She was engaged in an animated conversation with Emma, who had drawn some beautifully detailed scenes of a king, queen, and castle. Maybe Emma needed art lessons. Maybe that could be an outlet and talent that she could shine in.

The rest of the plane ride continued pretty smoothly. Hannah woke up. Lori listened to her lecture and gave her some pointers. Emma started crying later on. She was probably just

tired, but she claimed that she was starving and there was nothing that she liked to eat. She switched seats with Hannah so
that she was sitting near Lori, and then she finally fell asleep.
David engaged Hannah in conversation about the upcoming
events. It was clear that he'd read up about them as he spoke
excitedly with Hannah about what was going to take place.
Hannah seemed to appreciate his interest.

Slowly, everyone dozed off, until most of the plane was
asleep as they flew through the night.

Elaine shook Lori awake. "Lori, the plane will be landing
in a half hour."

Lori blinked a couple of times, trying to remember where
she was. She sat up straight.

"Make sure the kids' faces are washed and their hair is
brushed," Elaine was saying. "There will probably be reporters waiting to greet us at the airport."

Emma and Matthew were both still sleeping. David was
stretching. Hannah was reading her notes, once again. Sam
was drinking some water.

The plane finally landed and they exited the plane, not quite
knowing what to expect. Emma was still grouchy and Matthew
looked like he was half-asleep. Lori tried to make sure they all
looked presentable, but it wasn't easy after the long journey.

As they walked out of the security area, a large group was
standing with signs that read, "Welcome, Dr. Hannah Josephson!" Hannah walked over to the group and cameras started
flashing. People turned to look. Representatives of the Swedish
Ministry for Foreign Affairs, the American Embassy, and the
Nobel Prize committee were all there to greet Hannah and her
entourage. At first, no one noticed Lori, David, and the twins,

but suddenly someone pointed in their direction and before they knew it, cameras were flashing all around them, too.

After a few minutes in the airport, they were escorted outside, where a limousine was waiting to drive them to the Grand Hotel. Lori was in awe already. Matthew and Emma were quiet and seemed to be taking it all in. Emma loved the limousine.

They arrived at the hotel to find it bustling with people. New and old laureates and their families were arriving and being assigned to their rooms. Hannah's entourage was assigned four rooms and a suite with a kitchen. Lori and David took the twins and their suitcases up to the third floor, to their room. They opened the door and collapsed, exhausted, on the beds. It felt so good to lie down.

Emma ran to the window. "Look, Mommy and Daddy. I can see the palace!"

Lori stood up and walked to the window. The view was magnificent. There was a water inlet right outside the window and, sure enough, the royal palace was opposite the inlet. "David, you've got to come look!"

Now all four of them were standing at the window. David pointed. "Look, there's the Riksdagshuset, and there's the Royal Opera House!" The excitement was evident in his voice.

"And Lori, check out the information here," David called out again, motioning to a desk behind him.

Lori looked on the desk and found invitations and official instructions about where they should be and what they should wear for different events over the next four days. She read through them in amazement. There was also a pile of passes and tickets to all the tourist attractions in the city.

Lori inhaled deeply and looked up.

Dr. Wilson was staring at her. "Wow. All I can say is that all this is mind-blowing."

"And that was just the beginning."

"I'm interested in the ceremonial details, but also in your family interactions. I'm trying to process the talk that you had with your dad on the plane. That sounds like a great conversation."

"It was valuable to both of us. I never tried to imagine life from his perspective. It was interesting to change my frame of reference."

"Sometimes the spontaneous conversations are the most valuable."

"Yes, and I was fortunate that we had the conversation in a public place. Otherwise, I may have ended up saying things I wished I wouldn't have said, and I would never have heard how my father felt." Lori watched Dr. Wilson's facial expression. "But don't get too excited. Not all my family interactions were positive."

"As was to be expected," Dr. Wilson said. "Negative interactions can be learning experiences, too. It's all in what you make of them."

"That's what I need you for — to help me learn from the negative experiences." Lori paused and then quickly continued, "I should add that all in all, there were many more positive memories than negative, and I'm grateful for that. It was a wonderful experience, and I can't believe I ever considered missing it."

"You seem to be doing well, Lori." Dr. Wilson glanced at the clock. "I wish we had more time, but our session is up."

CHAPTER 22

D RIVING DOWN THE HIGHWAY IN his silver BMW, Tom tried to concentrate on the road instead of letting his mind wander. It was difficult. He was on his way to the hospital to meet with Allison's doctors together with Katie.

He had canceled all his morning appointments. Although Katie had told him it was unnecessary, he was intent on being at this meeting. He felt that Allison was at a very critical stage. He was beginning to resent the large amount of influence that Katie had on Allison's treatment compared to the minimal role he seemed to be playing. Not only was Katie making most of the decisions, she was leaving him out of the discussions, too. As Allison's dad, he wanted to be there to help make the decisions of where to go next.

To be fair, Tom understood why this had happened. As a successful pediatric urologist with a busy practice, he worked long hours. Katie, on the other hand, was a stay-at-home mom. She had the time and dedication to take Allison to all her appointments, to meet with all the therapists and doctors, and to research all the options. In the beginning, Tom trusted Katie. In retrospect, he realized that this was foolish. Not necessarily because Katie had made bad decisions, but because he was feeling more and more out of control in his ability to help Allison.

And help was what Allison needed. Why couldn't anyone help her? Tom slammed his hand on the dashboard. It wasn't fair! All they had to do was get her to eat, a normal animal instinctive behavior. What was so complicated about that?

This disease was ravaging Allison's body, and now it was ravaging Tom and Katie's marriage. They argued all the time. Forget about having a meaningful conversation — they rarely exchanged pleasant greetings. A second family tragedy was about as much as their marriage could handle. Tom was pretty sure that a divorce was looming in their future.

He pulled into the hospital's parking lot, and the hot August sun beat down on his balding head as he walked toward the hospital. He entered the main lobby and took the elevator up to the third floor. He had become very familiar with this building and felt right at home here. He was supposed to meet Katie outside the psychiatrist's office at ten forty-five.

Tom glanced at his watch. Ten fifty-two. Darn. Katie hated when he was late. Just another excuse for her to make a snide remark. He hustled down the hall. Sure enough, the door to Dr. Been's office was already open. Tom was sure that Katie would already be sitting inside. He poked his head in, and as he had predicted, there she was. She was made up perfectly, as usual. She looked pretty, but for some reason he was utterly not attracted to her. Even repelled. He walked in, ignoring Katie's glares. Megan, the nutritionist; Dr. McCartney, the pediatrician; and Dr. Jacobs, the therapist, were already sitting there, too.

Dr. Been motioned for him to have a seat. "Sorry it's a tight fit in here. We're just waiting for Dr. Isaacs, the GI. Oh, here he is now." Dr. Isaacs walked in and quickly took a seat.

Dr. Been cleared his throat and pushed his glasses up. "Well, we're here to discuss Allison's progress, a timetable for removing the nasogastric tube, and our plan going forward. Katie" — Dr.

Been looked at Allison's mother — "has expressed an interest in having the tube removed. We've talked about the need to keep it in until Allison reaches ninety pounds. There's no need to reiterate how dire a state she was in when she was admitted, due to her complete refusal to eat. However, we all recognize that using a nasogastric tube to feed her while keeping her arms in restraints is not a long-term solution."

Dr. McCartney and Dr. Jacobs were nodding in agreement. Tom was trying to stay focused, but his mind continued to wander. What if Allison really died? He didn't want to let himself go there, but he couldn't block the horrifying notion from filling his thoughts. Allison in a coffin. *No! Stop! Don't think it!* But it was too late. The picture of Allison, cold and motionless, lying alone in a wooden box, would not leave his thoughts.

Dr. Jacobs was speaking now about different therapy options, but Tom barely heard a word she was saying.

Suddenly, Katie interrupted, "Excuse me, can you be upfront with us and tell it to us straight? What is the likelihood of Allison dying? She just seems so out of it, and she seems to be getting worse and worse…"

The silence was palpable. Each of the doctors looked around the room, waiting for someone to take the lead. Finally, Dr. McCartney spoke up. "There is no scientific answer to that question. Allison is definitely battling for her life right now. I think that until she recognizes that we are her friends and anorexia is her enemy, instead of vice versa, her chances of surviving are not so great."

Tom spoke abruptly. "So what are you doing to help her recognize this? I mean, this is the twenty-first century! It seems like you should know how to get a kid to eat. What's so complicated about that?" His voice rose as spoke. He couldn't control his frustration and anger from seeping through. "Do you have a real plan, or are you just figuring it out as you go along?" Katie was giving him the glare again, but he didn't care.

Dr. Been looked at Tom. "Anorexia is one of the most painful and frustrating illnesses. You are completely right; it seems like it should be easy to overcome. All the person has to do is eat. And yet, I don't have to tell you how impossible that can be. It's torturous to look at Allison the way she is now. Do we have a plan? Yes, we have a plan." It was obvious that Dr. Been was trying to sound confident. He was not doing the best job. "Our first goal is to do whatever it takes to get her weight to at least ninety pounds. After that, we'll offer her all and any types of therapy — individual, art, group, family — in the hope that one of those will work." He looked at Dr. Jacobs. "Dr. Jacobs, do you want to add anything?"

Dr. Jacobs had a voice with a nasal quality, which grated on Tom's nerves. "You know, Allison has been very resistant to therapy. We can force the food in through the nasogastric tube, but we cannot force her to respond to therapy. There is a limit to how much we can do. At some point, Allison is going to have to take responsibility for conquering this disease. We are doing our best."

"Well, obviously, your best is not good enough!" Tom responded. "Don't talk to me about her taking responsibility for getting better. That just sounds like you're protecting yourselves."

Tom couldn't believe Dr. Jacobs had the audacity to say what she'd said. He could hear the despondency in her voice. She had given up on Allison. Written her off. Now she was just stalling, waiting for Allison to die so she could move on to the next patient.

Katie suddenly chimed in, still glaring at Tom. "Give them a break! Allison has been to three different hospitals, four different therapists, and a rehab program. You weren't there to watch how hard everyone tried. And so far, she hasn't responded to anyone."

Tom turned to Katie. "You couldn't handle it when that other therapist tried to put the blame on you, but you have no problem when Dr. Jacobs puts the blame on Allison?"

There was an awkward silence.

Katie's face turned bright red. "Oh, come on," she responded, and turned away.

Tom had gone too far. There was no point in arguing with Katie in front of all the doctors. He pushed back his chair and stood up. He looked around the room. Dr. Been was looking at him through his thick glasses with a concerned sort of look. Dr. Jacobs was just staring meekly. Megan was rubbing Katie's back. And the other doctors were looking down.

"If you don't mind, I'm going to take a little walk. I need some fresh air," Tom said. Everyone nodded or mumbled that it was okay.

Tom walked out of the office, closed the door, and punched his palm. He was annoyed at himself for making that last comment. He headed down the hallway toward Allison's room. Since he'd canceled all his morning appointments, he had some time to spare. He would go sit with Allison for a while and try to talk to her. He had better make the most of any time they had together.

CHAPTER 23

Now that Dr. Wilson knew who Hannah was, Lori felt strange talking about her. She felt like she was breaching the privacy of a celebrity. She was not sure how to resolve these feelings, and couldn't seem to shake them off as she entered Dr. Wilson's office.

"Hi, Lori," Dr. Wilson said, giving her his normal warm greeting.

"Hi," Lori replied, not knowing what else to say.

"So, have you gotten back into your normal schedule? Caught up on all your sleep?"

"Well, there are still a few days left of winter break. But we managed to have a really relaxing break, and I think everyone is back to normal."

"Are Emma and Matthew talking about their experiences?"

"I've been working on a scrapbook with them. It's a fun project to work on together, and it'll help them recall the vivid details of the events to share with their own children one day."

"You must have felt like a movie star for that week."

"Yes, I guess that's what it must feel like to attend the Oscars. I think Emma enjoyed it most. She said she felt like a princess. I enjoyed it because I knew it was temporary, but I would not want to live like that on a regular basis. Hannah was the one who surprised me the most. She usually hates publicity, but this time she seemed to enjoy the spotlight."

"Really?"

"Each day, there was a small army of news reporters outside our rooms. We thought it would annoy Hannah, but she would open her door and talk to them for a while — answering questions, explaining her work, and always inviting them to come back again later."

"She must have felt proud."

"Reporters were harping on the fact that Hannah's work for which she won the Nobel Prize was different from the work done by other scientists who won the Nobel Prize in Physics in the past. In recent years, most of the prizes awarded for physics were given to scientists who developed theoretical ideas, not practical experiments or inventions. However, Hannah's work has immediate implications; her theory and experiments are meant to impact droughts and water issues in the near future. The reporters bombarded her with questions about that.

"Hannah has strong positions on global warming and was thrilled to have a reason to articulate them to an audience who was lapping up every word. And then, of course, there was the fact that Hannah was a female physics Nobel Prize winner, a very rare commodity. Hannah is only the third woman in history to receive the Nobel Prize in Physics. Reporters asked some pointed questions about that. Hannah had a lot to say about discrimination of female scientists and the difficulty of combining a scientific career with raising children."

"It seems that Hannah got carried away with the global warming ideas."

"You must be referring to the major address she gave the afternoon after the Nobel ceremonies to the physics awarding institution."

"I guess so. I read reports about a speech that caused a small uproar."

"Well, Hannah made a reference that reporters interpreted as condemning the United States in their lack of efforts to curb global warming. People criticized that as unpatriotic."

"Did Hannah regret her comments?"

"Not that she admitted to any of us. She said that if it caused a renewed debate about what the US should be doing about global warming, she was happy to have caused the topic to be brought to the forefront." As Lori glanced down at her watch; she felt that she was wasting valuable time. There were more pressing issues that she wanted to discuss.

"So, where did we leave off last time?" Dr. Wilson seemed to be aware of Lori's desire to move on. He looked at his notes and then said, "You were talking about the first day that you arrived in Stockholm."

"Yes." Lori nodded. "Did I tell you that each laureate and family was assigned an attaché from the Swedish foreign office to serve as an escort and aide?"

Dr. Wilson shook his head.

"I think it'll be impossible for me to articulate the splendor and details of what went on throughout the week."

"When did the actual ceremonies begin?"

"The next day, Saturday, was the beginning of the events. Hannah spent Saturday attending a reception at the Nobel Foundation House, where she met all the other laureates. Then she attended a press conference at the Royal Swedish Academy of Sciences. Since we weren't invited to that, we used that time to sightsee. We used our free passes to go to a museum and to take a boat ride.

"On Saturday evening at the Grand Hotel, the faculty that awards the Nobel Prize for Physics gave a delightful dinner for the new physics laureates and any previous physics laureates who were in attendance. We attended that and enjoyed it immensely. Hannah had been nervous about getting along with John Kirby, the professor she was sharing the prize with, but that went great. No one would have known that there was any conflict between them. I had some intriguing discussions with a couple of previous laureates."

"And Emma and Matthew were able to sit through all this?"

"We had hired a nanny to watch them during the events that were not appropriate for them. She came with us to the dinner and took them back to the hotel room when they had enough. They were there for the beginning, but then went up to their room, watched a movie, and went to bed. It worked out well for us.

"The next day, December 10, was the principal day of the ceremonies. December 10 is actually the anniversary of the death of Alfred Nobel. Anyway, the invitations stated that the awards ceremony would take place from 4:00 to 6:30 p.m. at the Concert Hall, and then the banquet would take place in City Hall from 7:00 p.m. until 2:00 a.m. Hannah's day would begin at 10:30 a.m., at which time all the new and old laureates would go to Alfred Nobel's grave to lay wreaths of flowers. From there, she would be taken to the Concert Hall to practice with all the new laureates for the afternoon ceremony. After that, she would return to the hotel, eat a quick lunch, and then get dressed in her formal attire. We, on the other hand, were free until we had to dress in our gowns and tuxedos — at around 2:30 p.m.

"On Sunday morning, we were all up early, experiencing some nerves before the big event. Hannah was extremely anxious."

Lori, David, Hannah, Sam, Elaine, Emma, and Matthew were all sitting and eating a delicious breakfast in the private parlor of their hotel suite. Lori had a warm sensation of incredulousness.

She was reveling in the events that had taken place in the past couple of days and was anxiously anticipating the big events of the day. She slowly sipped her coffee. Emma and Matthew were eating scrambled eggs and toast. Lori's mom was pouring them orange juice.

"So, Emma and Matthew, what did you do yesterday morning?" Lori's mom smiled at them.

"Yes, where did you go? We didn't get to hear about your day," Lori's dad joined in.

Matthew started to answer when Hannah quickly interjected, "Mom and Dad, can you please not talk to Emma and Matthew right now?"

Elaine gave her a quizzical look.

"I'm very anxious right now. I have to practice my speech. I cannot have the kids talking, or it'll disturb me. Mom, Dad, I really need your help. Can you please talk to me, not the kids?"

Lori blurted out, "Hannah, what's the problem? The kids aren't disturbing you."

"Lori, I know you don't understand because you think your kids are the most wondrous creations, but I need you to get them out of here. I have to leave here at ten forty-five. From that time on, I'm basically busy until the ceremony. I need time without the kids around!" Hannah was talking quickly and avoiding eye contact as she spoke.

Lori felt her face burning. Emma and Matthew were staring at Hannah wide-eyed. Hannah was acting in a completely inappropriate manner. She could have said the same thing differently and Lori would have been sympathetic, but she was talking in an embarrassing and hurtful way in front of Emma and Matthew. Who knew what the twins were thinking? And what was that comment that Hannah had made about Lori thinking her kids were "the most wondrous creations"? Was she jealous that the twins were stealing attention from her? Was Hannah having a breakdown? Would she be able to attend the ceremonies in this state? Lori was simultaneously furious and puzzled by Hannah's odd behavior.

"I said get them out of here!" Hannah's voice was rising.

Lori's anger was increasing. Ignoring Hannah, she turned to her parents. "What's going on? Can you calm her down?"

"I'm sorry, Lori. Just take Emma and Matthew out." Elaine gave her an anxious, sad look.

Lori was ready to respond angrily, when David gently took her arm and said, "It's okay. Let's go."

Matthew started crying. "I'm not finished eating my eggs!" Emma just kept staring, her mouth hanging open.

Hannah was now acting almost insane. She was squeezing her eyes shut and rocking back and forth. "I need them out of here, I need them out of here…" she was mumbling over and over again.

Sam went over to her and hugged her sympathetically. "It's okay, Hannah. They're leaving."

Lori walked out of the room feeling sick to her stomach. What was going on? And why did her parents automatically side with Hannah? They always played into Hannah's behavior, and let her control them by her crazy outbursts. Lori was ready to catch the next plane home. She was wishing she had never agreed to come.

A few minutes later, after bundling up in their coats and hats, they exited the hotel. That was when Lori exploded. "David, that's it! Let's leave. I'm not attending the ceremonies after she treated me like that!" Lori felt her children's eyes on her, but she couldn't stop herself.

"Lori, try to stay calm. Hannah is obviously abnormal. Let's not make any rash decisions."

"Lori," Dr. Wilson interrupted, bringing Lori back to the present, "that sounds like a disaster. I thought that you said the trip went well."

"I'm not finished yet." Lori held up her arms, as if to gesture for Dr. Wilson to wait. "We walked to a café down the block. We bought the kids hot cocoas and cookies. I slowly calmed down. I tried to envision sitting with you at a therapy session. I reminded myself that the resentment I was feeling may actually be a defense to help alleviate the guilt I felt that my sister, the Nobel laureate, was so pathetic. I tried to explain this idea to David. He listened with empathy, and we talked in a way we hadn't talked in a long while. I remembered what I loved about him. I looked around and realized how fortunate I felt to have my wonderful family. Emma and Matthew were laughing together, seeming to have moved past the morning's traumatic interaction.

"Then I remembered another piece of wisdom you had given me at the last session: that when things got tense, I should try to look at the big picture. I envisioned what would happen if I ignored this incident. I realized that I could continue enjoying an extraordinary experience, and that Hannah would probably calm down and act more normally after she got through the ceremonies. If I stayed calm, Matthew and Emma would probably forget the little episode, too. When we finally left the café, I felt ready to go to the ceremonies. And I didn't feel anger toward Hannah or my parents."

"I'm so happy that you were able to do that." Dr. Wilson was beaming, "So now do I finally get to hear about the actual ceremonies? Or am I going to have to wait until next session?"

Lori looked at her watch. They had about five minutes left. "I couldn't describe it all in the time we have left. I hope you don't mind, but it'll have to wait until next time."

Dr. Wilson gave Lori a sheepish grin. "Hey, this is about you, not me. Sorry if I'm getting carried away with my excitement to hear your story."

Lori smiled back. "I understand."

"How about this question. Did Hannah ever apologize for her outburst?"

"No," Lori began, "but she acted overly kind the rest of the trip. And I'm convinced that it was because she felt bad about that morning. David and I agreed that she seemed to be trying to make things up to Emma and Matthew. She spent a couple of hours over a few different times sitting with Matthew, explaining all her experiments and work to him. He seemed to understand parts of it and enjoyed talking to her about it. She drew diagrams for him that he placed in a special folder. Since we've been home, he's been looking at them in bed every night before he falls asleep.

"But the kindest gesture she made involved Emma. On the day after the award ceremony, the royal family held an evening reception at the palace just for the new laureates and their spouses. Hannah got permission to bring a 'girlfriend' instead of a spouse — I'm sure the person she spoke to had assumed this girlfriend was her 'partner.' Then Hannah invited Emma to come with her. To Emma, this was a dream come true. She attended a divine reception in a palace with a king, queen, prince, and princesses!

"I was surprised in several ways. First of all, that Hannah recognized how excited Emma was about royalty. Second, that Hannah would do something so brash and daring, bringing a child with her to an event that was only open to laureates and their spouses. And finally, that Hannah was reaching out in such a significant way."

"Did the reception go well?"

"Hannah seemed really happy — maybe because she was able to make a child so happy. Emma was on cloud nine. She sat beside the queen for a little while. It was thrilling for her. I may venture to say that this was the highlight of her life so far! I have to admit that I did not think Hannah would be able to pull it off. I thought they would send Emma back, but it seems that everyone was pleasant and inviting to her."

"What an experience." Dr. Wilson said. "What was Matthew's highlight?"

"Matthew? Well, the day before our departure, we attended the Nobel Prize Concert at the Stockholm Concert Hall. Each year, the Nobel media arranges a concert. This year, cellist Yo-Yo Ma performed with the Royal Stockholm Philharmonic Orchestra. Matthew was mesmerized. He has recently developed an attraction to classical music. That's another thing that we have to start: Matthew now wants to take violin lessons."

"I love Yo-Yo Ma. That's awesome. Matthew and Emma sound like fascinating kids."

Lori gave Dr. Wilson a half smile.

Dr. Wilson looked back at Lori and then at the clock on the wall. "We better stop here, because now we've gone overtime."

"Thanks, Dr. Wilson. See you next time."

Lori stood up slowly, and walked out of the office. It was fun to relive the exciting events of the week by sharing them with someone.

CHAPTER 24

LORI ENTERED THE OFFICE. SHE had to remind herself of her goals before she got carried away talking about the ceremonies. There were two more events that Lori wanted help processing. She was looking forward to describing what took place at the awards ceremony, as well as the banquet that followed, but just had to keep in mind why she was here in the first place.

"Good afternoon, Lori."

"Hi, Dr. Wilson."

"How's everything going?"

"Nothing new and exciting right now. Everybody is back in school. We sent in Matthew's application to a school for gifted kids. We're going to check it out next week. And I signed Emma up for art lessons."

"Are you okay with the decision about the school?"

"Well, David and I have agreed that we are not making a decision yet. We're just looking into our options. You know me. I've done loads of research on the pros and cons of schools for gifted kids. As in everything, the answers are not simple. It seems that children who go to schools for the gifted are not necessarily more successful in their careers than children with similar IQs in regular schools. We've agreed that Matthew needs challenges and enrichment. We just have to decide which environment will be healthiest for him."

"That sounds good to me." Dr. Wilson nodded as he spoke.

No one spoke for a minute.

"Well?" Dr. Wilson looked at Lori.

"I'd love to continue describing the events of the ceremonies."

"I'm not stopping you."

After a stressful hour getting themselves and the kids dressed in their tuxedos and gowns, Lori and David were finally ready to leave to the Nobel Prize Awards Ceremony. Lori took one last glance at Emma and Matthew, making sure they looked suitable. As she did so, she sighed deeply. They both looked dazzling. Emma was wearing a delightful red gown with scattered beads sewn into it. She had chosen it herself and had the proudest expression on her face. Her long blond curls cascaded down her back, with small red flowers woven into the curls. Matthew looked almost as royal, in his black tuxedo with a red silk vest and bowtie to match Emma's gown. His serious demeanor went well with the look.

Emma ran to the bathroom mirror and peered at herself for the hundredth time. Matthew, growing impatient, said, "Let's go already! We're going to be late."

David said, "Matthew's right. C'mon everybody. Out the door!" Lori turned toward David, who looked rather handsome himself, also dressed in a black tuxedo, brown hair gelled up, and eyes as piercingly blue as always.

Lori took Emma's and Matthew's hands in hers and walked toward the door. Then, almost as if he hadn't realized what he had seen the first time, David turned back once more and looked right at Lori. "Wow. You look magnificent." And she did. Her chocolate brown gown with its full-length skirt swished as she moved. Its flutter sleeves made Lori feel like a princess herself. Her blond hair was blow-dried straight, but set with some curls at the bottom.

Lori smiled back at David, loving the fact that he could not stop staring. "Let's go," she said. David took Emma's hand in his, and they all walked out the door together. As they exited the room, Lori could not help reverting her thoughts to what had happened with Hannah earlier in the day. She hoped it would not be awkward being with her.

But Lori had nothing to worry about. As soon as she and her family entered the hotel hallway, they were met by attachés from the Swedish foreign office. These attachés were waiting to escort Hannah and all her accompanying guests to the awards ceremony. There was no time to ponder on earlier events, no time to even say hello. Before Lori could catch her breath, they were all on their way out of the Grand Hotel, along with Hannah and her parents. Lori looked around in amazement at the crowds of people lining the streets to honor the laureates.

They reached the Concert Hall and entered with Hannah. Even greater numbers of people were standing in the square outside the hall. Lori looked toward Hannah in awe. Suddenly, Lori realized how proud she felt to be her sister. She looked toward her parents and saw sheer joy on their faces. Instead of feeling jealous, she felt a sincere surge of happiness for Hannah, her parents, and, surprisingly, herself.

At this point, the laureates had to meet on the mezzanine floor to line up, while family members and all attending guests were making their way to their seats in the auditorium. As Hannah turned to go, Lori quickly whispered, "Good luck!"

Lori, her parents, David, Emma, and Matthew were escorted into the main hall. Lori's eyes opened wide. The auditorium was packed with about 1,500 people, many of whom were celebrities. It was decorated exquisitely, filled with flowers that Lori had been told were sent from the city of San Remo, Italy, where Alfred Nobel spent his final years. There were numerous types of flowers, including roses and orchids all woven together in intricate arrangements.

They were led to their seats in the front row. David looked at Lori, as if to say, *Can you believe this?* The front row had seating on the left and right designated for family members of the new laureates. The next three rows were designated for the prime minister, the cabinet, and the diplomatic corps.

At four o'clock promptly, a fanfare of trumpets blared loudly, announcing the entry of the king and royal family. The Royal Stockholm Philharmonic Orchestra played "The King's Anthem," as the royal family proceeded to their seats on stage. As soon as the royal family was seated, another loud fanfare blared, which was the signal for the laureates to make their entrance. Uniformed ushers slowly opened two tall doors at the rear of the stage. As the orchestra played music, the king and all assembled rose, and the laureates marched onto stage, to the left of the royal family. They stood for a moment in front of the red chairs on which they were to sit, made a reverence to the king, and sat down.

Seated on the stage were also about ninety members of the Royal Swedish Academy of Sciences, the Nobel Assembly of Karolinska Institutet, the Board of Directors of the Nobel Foundation, and the previous laureates who were in attendance. Lori kept her eyes on Hannah, trying to read her expression.

Was Hannah anxious? It was hard to tell; she sat there almost expressionless.

Yet, as Lori continued to look, she could detect the smallest smile emerging from the corner of Hannah's lips, diminishing the severity her thin face and high cheekbones often implied. Still, even in her moment of glory, she looked just like Hannah. She was dressed up just enough to be appropriate without being elaborate; she was wearing a simple black velvet top and long black silk skirt, with a touch of makeup, and glasses. Lori had tried to convince her to get contacts for the event, but Hannah was never one to value style over comfort.

As Lori continued to absorb every minute detail, she realized that she was actually trembling. She looked at David. He was so engrossed in the events that he didn't notice her looking at him. She looked at Matthew and Emma. They, too, had their eyes opened wide in amazement. She looked at her parents. They seemed to be beside themselves with pride.

The ceremony began with the king welcoming each recipient. Then the president of the Nobel Foundation welcomed the royal family and guests and briefly reviewed the life of Alfred Nobel. Although he spoke in Swedish, Lori was able to follow along by reading the address, which was printed in English, along with a few other languages, in the program book.

Since the prizes were awarded in the order noted in Nobel's will, the physics prize was the first to be awarded. Lori felt her heart beating faster. Finally, the moment they had been waiting for all this time! Hannah Josephson and John Kirby arose for their citation. They walked slowly toward the king, as the trumpeters sounded another fanfare. The king, the auditorium guests, and the other laureates on stage all rose in a standing ovation. This was too much for Lori and she began to cry softly, overcome with emotion.

Emma turned toward her mother and whispered. Lori couldn't hear what she was saying, but she read her lips: "Why are you crying?"

"I'm so happy," Lori mouthed back. Emma shrugged and turned her attention back toward the proceedings. In truth, Lori was not sure why she was crying. Was it sheer happiness that brought these tears to her eyes? Did she finally appreciate all the difficulties and painful moments Hannah had experienced? Was she crying from the elation of knowing that Hannah finally had her moment of joy?

Or was it painful memories that brought these tears to her eyes? Was she thinking of all the difficult moments she had experienced so that Hannah could have this night? Or was it deeper than that? Was it overwhelming feelings of the fleeting-ness of life that brought these tears? Watching humans being awarded prizes for helping humanity made Lori think about life and death, reasons for living, the meaningfulness or meaning-lessness of life. Could humanity actually accomplish anything? Her mind was spinning out of control.

Lori turned her focus back to the events unfolding before her. Hannah was just accepting the diploma and medal. Her face beaming, she turned toward Lori and seemed to give her a wink. Then Hannah and John returned to their seats.

It was odd to see Hannah as a respected individual being honored by the world. It was hard to believe that this was her sister, the same Hannah whom Lori had seen in her worst and most pathetic moments. It was strange to think that the world had no idea who the true Hannah was. Or maybe it was the world who knew who the true Hannah was, and it was Lori who had never known. David gave Lori's hand a little squeeze. Hannah was officially a Nobel laureate, an achievement that could never be taken away from her. Lori breathed in deeply and tried to make sense of it all.

"What a spectacular event!" Dr. Wilson was obviously enjoying hearing about this.

"There were still hours more. As soon as all the laureates had received their diplomas and medals, the awards ceremony was over, and it was time for the banquet. Cars came to take all of us to Stadshuset, Stockholm City Hall. City Hall was decorated breathtakingly, too, with stunning, ingenious floral arrangements. We, the guests, were seated in the Blue Hall. Then, the guests of honor, including Hannah, were introduced by trumpeters dressed in medieval garb as they made their way down the grand stairway to their seats. Members of the royal family escorted the Nobel laureates. King Carl Gustaf himself escorted Hannah. They walked arm-in-arm down the stairs, and this time Hannah's smile filled her face.

"David, Emma, Matthew, and I were seated at a table with a great-great-niece of Alfred Nobel. We enjoyed conversing with her. The banquet began, and I have to tell you that I've never eaten like that or been served like that in my life, and I'm sure I never will be again. There were more than thirty chefs in the kitchen cooking the most exquisite, elegantly decorated, and delicious food. Over two hundred waiters and waitresses worked with military precision. For each new course, the waiters would appear on the balcony and wait for the orchestra to begin playing music. Then they would march in formation down the marble stairs to their assigned tables.

"At the beginning of the banquet, a toast was proposed for His Majesty, King Carl Gustaf, and another toast was proposed in memory of Alfred Nobel. Between courses, there was a main address to welcome the laureates. There was also entertainment provided by the Royal Swedish Ballet. Throughout and after dinner, one new laureate from each prize category gave an acceptance speech. This was the event that Hannah had been dreading. I'm not sure why she didn't have John Kirby give the speech if she was so nervous about it, but I'm sure it was a complicated decision.

"When her turn came, I was sweating profusely. My parents were sitting at another table and I couldn't see them. Hannah had to rise from the head table, walk up eleven marble stairs to a rostrum on the first landing, and then turn and face the remarkable assemblage of royalty, celebrities, and previous laureates. As she walked up the stairs, my breathing came heavier. David whispered to me, 'Calm down!' and we both giggled, which helped me relax.

Hannah began speaking and I could hear her voice shaking. I thought it was going to be a disaster, but as she progressed, her voice grew stronger and she actually spoke well. Once that was over, I was able to enjoy myself much more.

"Dessert was the highlight of the evening. All the lights in the hall were turned off. The orchestra began playing a lively tune, as the waiters appeared on the balcony carrying trays of sculptured ice cream that were illuminated. The trays also held ice sculptures of different figures such as City Hall, and letters spelling the names of different categories of prizes. Each ice figure was illuminated by different colored light bulbs that were powered by batteries frozen inside the ice. It was a phenomenal sight. As we ate dessert, the choir sang lovely songs. Finally, the choir marched down the marble stairs singing their final song, and the banquet ended at eleven thirty."

"Did Emma and Matthew make it until the end?"

"Barely. They were both dozing off at the table, so at that point we sent them back to the hotel with the nanny. At eleven thirty, there was a general reception in the gold room. And then, after midnight, there was dancing until about two in the morning. I felt like I was Cinderella at the ball. I was in total awe. I felt like the clock was going to strike midnight, and I'd realize that I did not belong.

"As David and I danced, I felt madly in love and like life couldn't be more perfect. David and I had to keep pinching ourselves to believe that we were really here and part of this."

"I never realized the extent of what went on at the ceremonies."

"I know. I don't think many people do."

"So how was your relationship with Hannah the next day? Did everything truly return to normal?"

"Well, we all slept late. Then, at two o'clock in the afternoon, Hannah gave her major address before the physics awarding institution. We all attended her speech. That was the controversial speech that you read about. When it was over, she was bombarded with reporters.

"The day after that, there was a guided tour of Stockholm, along with a visit to the National Museum of Fine Arts for all laureates and their family members. This was a relaxed and fun time for all the families and guests to spend time together. Emma and Matthew were getting along well with the other children. David was taking everything in, loving all the interesting places and people he was experiencing. I was becoming friends with the economics prize winner. A grandfather in his eighties, he had fascinating life insights and an interesting life story. But I'm getting off topic.

"Later that night, at ten thirty, I was sitting in our hotel room, relaxing. My parents, David, and Matthew had conked out, exhausted.

I thought Hannah was sleeping, too."

Lori was sipping a tea, enjoying the silence after all the craziness of the past few days. There was so much to think about — wonderful events to rehash and experiences to process. Just then, she heard the doorknob turn. Hannah entered the parlor, wearing her bathrobe.

"Hi, Lori." Hannah sat down beside her.

"It's hard to believe this is all almost over. Isn't it?" Lori said.

"Our fairy tale is about to end."

"If only it could be 'happily ever after,'" Lori mused.

"Yeah. Well, I think I've come to realize that the joys of life are only joys because there are also sorrows. So I guess there can never be a 'happily ever after.'"

"That was profound, Hannah," Lori said, the surprise evident in her tone.

Hannah shrugged. Lori was enjoying this rare, pleasant moment alone with her sister.

"Anyway, Lori, there's something I wanted to..." Hannah struggled to find the words.

Lori's heart beat a little faster. What could Hannah be about to tell her? This had the makings of a disaster.

"You know, the laureates are allowed to purchase three replicas of lesser value of the gold medals we receive. Many laureates donate their replicas to the institutions of higher education where they studied."

"Yes?" Lori was still not sure where this conversation was headed. Or, more accurately, she couldn't believe what she was guessing Hannah might say.

"I haven't received the replicas that I ordered yet, but I want you to know that I'm planning on giving one to you," Hannah finished off, the words tumbling out of her mouth.

Lori looked at Dr. Wilson. "You'll never believe the emotion that I felt when Hannah told me this."

"Can I guess?"

"Sure."

"Anger."

"How do you do that? You're really good; I was burning with rage! It seemed so paradoxical that this gesture of kindness would make me so angry. Why did you guess that?"

"Lori, look at the pattern of your life and you'll see that it is obvious."

"Well, as usual, you're right on target. At first, I felt so angry I was ready to explode. I was sure Hannah was doing this to rub in how much greater she was than me, that she wanted to give me a medal to display so I would have a constant reminder that she was better. But then, Dr. Wilson, I thought of you. I told myself that this anger must be a defense. What could it be a defense for? My mind spun.

"Then I knew. I felt guilty taking this medal from her because I felt like I'd never done anything for her, other than bitterly resent the honor she had received her whole life. I'd spent so much time being angry that I could never get my parents' attention like she did, that I never had the energy to be kind to Hannah. And now, she was reaching out to me, trying to repay the kindnesses that sisters are supposed to bestow on one another. The problem was that there was no kindness to repay. I felt overwhelmed with the realization that I had never done anything for Hannah.

"You know…" Lori's voice cracked. She swallowed hard. "I suddenly realized that we're all Hannah really has. My parents won't live forever, and then who will Hannah have left? She has some friends — some colleagues whom she considers close acquaintances. But she lives a pretty isolated life. Who really cares about her?" Lori swallowed a couple more times.

"So how did you respond to Hannah's gesture?"

"I took a minute to gain my composure. Then I thanked her profusely and told her how deeply touched I was."

Dr. Wilson looked at Lori intently.

"So, Dr. Wilson, how do I overcome this guilt?"

"How do you move past this guilt? You must have thought about it a lot."

"Yes, I have."

"Have you come up with anything?"

Lori should have known that Dr. Wilson would not let her get away with having him solve her problem. "As I'm sitting here and relaying these events to you, I guess I'm realizing that this is Hannah's way of showing me that she really wants a relationship with me, that she wants to be friends. All I have to do is accept the medal. That, in itself, is a kindness. And then, try to be friends back." It all seemed so clear sitting in Dr. Wilson's office, articulating these thoughts. Real life made things turn fuzzy.

"I'm sure you know it won't be easy 'being friends.' But she took the first step. And I guess if you're creative, you'll think of ways to take the second."

Lori suddenly felt obliged to add another piece of information. "The truth is, I've been realizing that often when David demonstrates gestures of kindness, I get mad, too. I think it stems from that same guilt thing about not deserving kindness. I use the anger as a defense to protect myself, to prove I don't deserve it, or at least sabotage it."

"That certainly fits the pattern."

Lori waited for Dr. Wilson to say more. But he just sat quietly, almost smiling. So Lori continued, "I've been working on this, and our relationship is feeling…healthier than it has in years."

"Great to hear."

Lori looked at Dr. Wilson, appreciating his approval, and then continued, "Once again, you've come through. Thanks for everything."

"Lori, you're an easy client. For the most part, you're willing to accept anything I present to you. You take what I say to heart and are able to apply it to your life. In this way, you've taught me many things and have enriched my life. I owe you a thank-you, too. I have only grown in my respect for you in these last few months."

Lori blushed uncomfortably. It was hard to know if Dr. Wilson was sincere. She quickly changed the topic. "I have one more issue that I need help resolving. This one has to do with my mother." Glancing at her watch, she quickly added, "So I'll start with that next session."

Dr. Wilson stood up and then turned to Lori. "So what did you do with the medal?"

"I haven't received it yet, but I'll display it on the wall in our living room. It's a great conversation piece and something that I'm proud of."

Dr. Wilson smiled. "I think that shows something about your emotional healing — that you're able to display the medal in a prominent place."

Lori stood up, too. "Yes, I agree with your assessment." She smiled back and then turned to leave.

CHAPTER 25

ORI WONDERED WHAT DR. WILSON would say about this next problem. It didn't seem like there was anything he or she could do. She just didn't think his wise words could bring a solution this time. Still, Lori was sure of one thing: Without the past few months of therapy, this dilemma would not have been the mere difficulty it was presenting itself as now; it would have been an utter disaster, with devastating and profound implications.

As Lori entered the office, Dr. Wilson called out his usual greeting. Lori responded in kind. Suddenly, Lori felt invaded. Why did this stranger sitting in front of her know her innermost and deepest quandaries? She had no idea why she felt an intense desire to keep her thoughts private. But she breathed in slowly and reminded herself that all this therapy had been helping her tremendously.

Dr. Wilson looked down at his notes. "Anything new this past week?"

"It's been pretty calm. The kids actually got along really well. I wonder if it has to do with my new sense of calmness."

"That sounds positive."

"So last week I started to tell you about a problem I had with my mother."

"Yes." Dr. Wilson gave Lori one of his quizzical looks and waited.

"It was on the morning before our departure. Hannah had attended some luncheon — maybe at the American Embassy? I can't remember exactly. My dad and David had taken the twins on an outing to a science museum or something. My mom and I wanted to spend some time together. We hadn't done anything like that in years. We decided to take a walk through the streets of Stockholm. Everything was going well, until the end."

Lori and her mom had enjoyed a lovely walk. It was cold outside, but since they were bundled up in coats, hats, and gloves, the air felt good. They stopped in various interesting shops and boutiques, and bought a few souvenirs. Finally, they sat down to drink a hot coffee and buy a small lunch. Lori really liked these European cafés.

She was feeling a sense of contentment and happiness that she couldn't remember feeling before. The week had been mostly a dream. With only a few bumps, it had been a wonderful experience, unlike anything she could have imagined. She was feeling extra confident, as she thought about how her relationship with Hannah seemed to be mending, and about the great conversation with her father on the plane ride.

"Lori," her mom interrupted her thoughts, "you look so serious. What's on your mind?"

Lori suddenly had an inspiration. Maybe now was the time to make the healing complete. She knew she had to start speaking before she chickened out, so she forced the words out of her mouth before she could think too carefully about what she was about to do. "Mom, you know, there is something…"

Elaine looked at her. Lori didn't like the look, but she pressed on. "I…I…you know, once, well…" she found herself stumbling over her words, but she persisted. "When I was nine, you were out one afternoon and Grandma was watching me. I was looking for some dress-up clothes, when I found some old notebooks of yours." The look on her mom's face was getting more intense. "I...read through some of them. There was one that really disturbed me. I've always felt bad about it, even until this day."

Lori waited for her mom to comment, but she just sat in stony silence. There was no stopping now, so with no other choice, Lori kept going. "It was an entry you wrote when you found out you were pregnant with me. You wrote how disappointed you were, that the pregnancy was a mistake..." The desperation was evident in Lori's voice.

"You read through my private papers?!" Elaine was livid.

"I was a kid, Mom." Lori's voice grew weak. She felt like a kid again, right now. A kid being admonished by her mother.

"You violated my privacy and now you want my sympathy? Sorry, Lori, I have nothing to say!"

Lori was numb. After all these years of trying to acquire the courage to tell her mom what she had read, after all those nights of dreaming of her mom hugging her and telling her that she was so sorry, that she never meant it — this was how the conversation had gone? Lori was too frozen to do anything.

Elaine stood up. "I'm tired. Let's go back to the hotel."

Lori got up, too. Her face was burning. They walked in silence, until Elaine broke it by bringing up some logistics that had to be worked out for the trip home. Lori didn't know what to make of their disastrous conversation. She tried to act as normal as she could.

When David and the twins got back, David could tell immediately that something was up. He turned on the TV for the kids and then sat down next to Lori, who was sitting on the bed with a frown on her face.

"You don't look well. Is everything all right?"

Lori shrugged slightly. She couldn't even admit to David how hurt she was. It was too painful. "I tried to talk to my mom about the resentments of my youth, but she just brushed it off."

"Lori, you know that this was a silly time to bring it up! This is a week to celebrate Hannah's astounding achievements. You should have waited until everything calms down."

Lori said quietly, "Yeah, I don't know what I was thinking. And thanks for being so sympathetic."

"Are you being sarcastic?"

"Yes, I am being sarcastic!" Lori raised her voice, but then she calmed down quickly. "I'm sorry. I'm just tired and edgy right now. Let's stop this conversation."

David shrugged and turned away.

Lori looked at Dr. Wilson. "The amazing thing is that I'm not as devastated as I imagined I would have been. I was really upset for the next couple of hours, but then somehow it seemed much less significant than it should have. Look, I can even talk about it now without getting emotional." Lori stopped and contemplated what she was saying. "Do you think I'm in denial? That I'm really harboring intense feelings inside?"

"Slow down. Let's go back a little. That conversation sounds awful." This time, Dr. Wilson took a deep breath. "Did you tell David the details of the conversation on a later occasion?"

"Actually, I did. A few nights after we got home. He apologized for brushing me off and was much more sympathetic."

"If you had not told him the specifics of the conversation, I'd be more concerned that you were harboring inner emotions. Why do you think you're calm about this disastrous reaction from your mother?"

Lori thought carefully before replying. "The truth is, I think that even though my mom did not react in the way that I had hoped, there was still therapeutic benefit to the conversation."

"What do you mean?"

"Let me think about how I can articulate what I'm thinking."

"Take your time, Lori."

She closed her eyes for a few seconds. "I feel good that my mom finally knows how bad I felt by what she wrote. Even if she didn't react by apologizing, it just feels good that she knows what I went through. Upon contemplation, I think I realized that the fact that she reacted so harshly shows how seriously she took my words. If she didn't feel bad, she wouldn't have reacted like that. And the bottom line is, I got a load off my chest. There's no longer a painful secret between my mother and me." Lori looked to Dr. Wilson, waiting for his agreement.

"Well, like you said, it would've been the perfect storybook ending if she could have said, 'Lori, I'm so sorry you read that. We loved you more than anything from the moment you were born. I should have burned that diary entry!' But you can never control other people's reactions. And, like you said, the positive part of your conversation is that you no longer have to have this horrible secret bottled up inside you." Dr. Wilson stopped talking for a brief moment. "Lori, I'm impressed. You've come so far in your ability to move past negative interactions."

Lori grinned. She felt good. It was interesting that when she had come to therapy this afternoon, she had felt as though there was nothing that Dr. Wilson could say that could fix the difficult situation that she had gotten into with her mother. He hadn't said anything profound, but as he had guided her through understanding her feelings, he'd helped her feel better.

"So were those the highlights of your family interactions on the trip?"

"I think that, for the most part, I've relayed all the noteworthy events." Lori looked away. "It's strange how significantly this Nobel Prize has affected my personal life. Isn't it? It caused me to go to therapy, and it forced me to deal with so many issues that I had tucked away for many years."

"I guess you feel happy about it now."

"Oh, yes. I most definitely do."

"And Hannah's life? It must have affected her."

"That's a given. She has been bombarded from all over with requests for interviews and speeches. She's received job offers from numerous prestigious universities."

"Will she accept a new job?"

Lori shrugged. "I don't know. I called her a couple of times since the ceremonies, but it hasn't been easy to get through to her."

"How did the week end?"

"Hannah had some more dinners and luncheons to attend. We went to some of them. One in particular was very enjoyable. It was hosted by a professor of physics from some prestigious Swedish university. There were three or four other local professors, along with their spouses and children. Matthew and Emma enjoyed playing with all the kids. There were also three young physics students there. It was fun meeting and conversing with all these people.

But what was truly amazing was watching Hannah. She seemed so confident; she gave off an aura of... I don't know exactly how to describe it, except that she had a presence. It was obvious that everyone around her had the utmost respect for her. It was a good experience for me to see her in that light. I felt myself developing a newfound respect for her as the week drew to a close."

Lori stopped and then added, "Throughout the week, many people asked me what it was like growing up as her younger sister."

"How did you respond to that?"

"I guess I tried to make a joke of it. I talked about what it was like being known as Hannah's younger sister. But I'd always add that, all kidding aside, I was really proud to be her sister."

"Did you mean it?"

"I think so. Hannah would smile when I said that, and I think she appreciated it." Lori paused for a brief moment and then continued, "My mom and dad would tell stories about what a genius Hannah was from the time she was an infant. That was more painful to endure."

"Why?"

"I guess because it reminded me of how hurtful it felt that the focus of my parents' entire existence was on her." It was fascinating to note how easily Lori was now able to express this.

"I understand."

"Another interesting experience took place at the National Museum. One night late in the week, we were all invited to a lovely musical program there. Hundreds of Stockholm's citizens came to greet the laureates. The Academic Choir of Stockholm sang riveting songs while an orchestra played. Afterward, a buffet supper was served in a room in the museum. For some reason, I particularly enjoyed this event. We were all laughing and joking around."

"It sounds like it was a less stressful event — not too much pressure and no expectations."

"You're probably right." Lori looked out the window. "So that's that. Thanks for helping me process all of that."

CHAPTER 26

L ORI PULLED INTO HER DRIVEWAY. It was 5:30 p.m. and she was returning from work. She stopped in front of her mailbox and took out the mail. She glanced through it and suddenly stopped. That was odd. She ripped open the envelope as she sat back down in her car. As she read through the letter, a slow grin spread across her face. She couldn't wait to show it to David. And, of course, Dr. Wilson.

Lori pulled up to the garage, pushed the garage clicker, and waited for the door to open. Then she pulled into the garage and got out of her car. As she opened the door to the house, Matthew came running to greet her. "Hi, Mommy! Daddy's making hot dogs for dinner."

"David, hi! You'll never believe what I got in the mail," Lori called out.

"Lori?" David came walking toward her. Slowly.

Lori stopped short. David looked worried. Really worried.

"David! Is something wrong?"

David motioned his head toward Matthew. "Can you come upstairs for a moment?"

"Okay." Lori's heart started to beat faster.

She followed David upstairs. "David! What's going on?" The panic in Lori's voice was obvious.

"Nothing horrible. Don't worry," David said, but Lori didn't believe him.

"Just spit it out already."

"Your dad just called. Apparently, Hannah overdosed on some medication. She's in critical but stable condition."

Lori's head was pounding. Everything was blurry. "What are you talking about? Do you mean to tell me she... she tried to... commit suicide? Will she be okay?" Lori put her hands to her head.

"Your dad wants you to fly out there immediately."

"Does that mean things are worse than he's saying? What do I do? Can you help me get plane tickets?" Lori's breathing came hard and fast. Why would Hannah do this now? After all the wonders of Stockholm, she should be on a high! *Oh, Hannah, what were you thinking?*

An hour later, Lori was in the car on the way to the airport. Miraculously, she'd managed to get a plane ticket. Then she had thrown some things in a bag and run out of the house. David wanted to drive her to the airport, but she assured him she'd be fine. She was thinking faster than she could process everything. She desperately wanted to speak to Dr. Wilson. She knew that she could call him if it was an emergency, but she decided she would first try doing this herself.

She started by concentrating on deep breathing. Then she asked herself what emotion she was feeling. It was hard to think straight, but she forced herself to concentrate. Okay. She felt angry, as usual. And she felt guilty, as usual.

Why did she feel angry? She was angry because, because... She tried to think. Because, once again, Hannah needed attention. She needed everyone to focus on her. She missed all the attention of the prize ceremonies, so she had to do this so people would give her attention again. Lori was angry that Hannah had done something so horrible in order to be noticed.

Lori tried to ask herself if these feelings were rational. No, they were not. If Hannah had succeeded in killing herself, she'd get no attention, because she would be dead. Dead people cannot feel attention.

Why did she feel guilty? She felt guilty because… That was easy. She felt guilty because maybe there was something she had done at the ceremonies that had sparked this. Maybe she made Hannah feel bad by rubbing in how lonely she was with no family of her own. Maybe that's what caused this attempted suicide.

Oh, please G-d, were Lori's next thoughts, *make it only be an attempted suicide, not a suicide. Please G-d, make her be okay. She's such a good person. She tries so hard. She has so much to offer to humanity. Don't let her die!* Lori's thoughts were rambling, but she tried to stay in control.

Were these guilty feelings rational? No! Lori had tried her best to share what she had with Hannah. She couldn't feel bad that her own life was working out for her, that she had a husband and kids whom she loved. She'd made a promise that she would try to share this with Hannah. She could not be expected to do more.

So what was Lori going to say to Hannah when she saw her? Again, her next thought was: *Please, G-d, let her be alive!*

CHAPTER 27

LORI PULLED UP TO DR. Wilson's office. It was hard to believe so much had happened since their last session.

"Lori, how are you doing?" Dr. Wilson greeted Lori as she entered the office.

"It's been a very difficult week for me. You won't believe what happened." Lori rubbed her eyes.

"Really?" Dr. Wilson leaned in, interested in what she was going to say.

"It all began when I returned from work on Monday. David greeted me by telling me that Hannah was in critical condition. As far as he had heard, she'd tried to commit suicide."

"What?" Dr. Wilson's shock was obvious.

"I caught the first flight I could find."

Lori was in sitting a cab on her way to the hospital. It was ten thirty at night, and she had no idea what to expect when she got there. She had been trying to call her parents' cell phones nonstop since her plane landed, but no one was answering the phone. In the pit of her stomach, Lori was harboring an intense fear that Hannah had died. What would she do if Hannah died? It wasn't fair! She was just beginning a new relationship with her. Why did Hannah have to do that?

The cab driver interrupted her thoughts. "We're here, ma'am."

Her mind clearly on other things, she pulled out some cash and paid him. Then she grabbed her small suitcase and walked into the hospital.

"Excuse me, where is the ICU?" she asked at the information desk.

"Third floor. Elevators to your right."

"Thank you."

Lori walked into the elevator. Her heart was pounding as she wondered what she would find when she got upstairs.

As she exited the elevator, she saw a main desk. Walking briskly, she hurried to the nurses' station.

"Excuse me. I'm looking for Hannah Josephson. Do you know her room number?"

"First of all, visiting hours are over for tonight."

"Oh, right." Lori forgot about that.

"But I'll check what room she is in."

The nurse scanned the computer. After a few tense moments, she said, "I'm sorry. Hannah Josephson is no longer here."

Lori's heart was beating so loud, she thought it might explode. She felt a lump forming in her throat. *Hannah's dead? Noooooo!* is what she wanted to scream.

The nurse continued, "Ms. Josephson has been moved out of the ICU into a regular room. Her new room number is 507."

Lori slowly let out her breath. *Hannah's going to be okay. Hannah's going to be okay.* She repeated these words in her head, savoring each one of them.

She took the elevator up to the fifth floor. The nurses at the nurses' station stopped her as she tried to enter the ward.

"Sorry. Visiting hours are up."

"I'm here to see my sister, Hannah Josephson. Do you know

if her parents are around?"

"I'll call them." The nurse walked off.

Lori sat down on one of the chairs in the waiting room. After what seemed like hours, but must have been five minutes, Lori saw her mom walking toward her.

"Lori!" Elaine came running and embraced Lori in a tight hug.

They both started sobbing. After they calmed down somewhat, her mom gave her some information. "Hannah was just moved out of intensive care a couple of hours ago. It seems like she has pulled out of the danger zone."

"Thank G-d! When can I see her?"

"Well, I don't think they'll let you in tonight. Anyway, right now she's sleeping."

"What happened?" Lori blurted out.

Her mom shrugged. "We don't know. Hannah hasn't been able to tell us yet."

"Who found her?"

"She was supposed to call me to give me some information about something. When she didn't call, I tried to call her and couldn't get through. I called her office, and her secretary told me she hadn't shown up for work this morning. I tried calling her numerous times, but couldn't reach her. I was worried. Dad thought I was being ridiculous.

"Finally, I called her neighbor and asked her to check in on Hannah. She didn't call back for forty-five minutes. When she finally called, she said that she'd found the door unlocked, so she walked in. She found Hannah lying on the floor with a bottle of pills beside her. She called the paramedics, waited until they arrived, and then called me back.

"When we heard that, Dad and I panicked, as I'm sure you can imagine. We tried desperately to speak with someone at the hospital who could answer our questions, but no one seemed to know if she'd be okay. We jumped in the car to make the three-hour drive, calling the hospital from our cell phones constantly. When we finally arrived, we saw Hannah, alive. The doctors said they thought she would be fine, although they wouldn't know if there was permanent damage until she woke up."

"Why didn't you tell me that before my trip here? I spent the whole plane ride thinking that Hannah might be dying!"

"Sorry. I thought Dad gave you the message. Anyway, it's been traumatic nonetheless."

"What did Hannah say since she woke up?"

"Not that much. She seems embarrassed. I'm sure she'll talk more tomorrow."

"So do you have any ideas where I should sleep tonight?" Lori suddenly realized how tired she was.

"Oh, of course. There's a hotel across the street. Dad and I will take care of the bill."

"Please, Mom. That isn't necessary. I'm exhausted, so I'm going to check in. I'll be back tomorrow morning."

"Come first thing. Hannah really wants to see you."

Lori felt odd when she heard her mom say those words. Why would Hannah really want to see her? Maybe her mom was just saying that. "Of course, I'll be here first thing. Where else do I have to go? Where are you guys sleeping?"

"I think we're just going to sleep on these chairs in the waiting room."

Lori shrugged. She could understand why they wanted to do that. "See you tomorrow morning."

Lori collapsed on the bed as soon as she checked in. Lying in her clothes, she called David, who had been waiting anxiously to hear from her. He told her that the kids went to bed relatively easily, although they wanted to know where Lori went and if Aunt Hannah would be okay. Lori had no energy to talk, so she said she would call back after she visited with Hannah the next morning.

Lori woke up at 6:45 a.m. Still dressed in her clothes from the previous day, she felt groggy and achy. She jumped into the shower, wondering what time visiting hours began at the hospital. After she was dressed, she called the hospital. They told her visiting hours didn't begin until nine o'clock. She had an hour and a half to wait.

There was a Starbucks in the lobby, so she took her purse, walked downstairs, ordered a coffee, and sat down with *The New York Times*. She sat there for forty-five minutes. Then she called David, who said he got the kids off to school and everything was fine. With nothing else to do, she walked over to the hospital and stopped in the gift shop. She picked out a nice card for Hannah. Then she called her mom, who said Hannah was up and was anxiously awaiting her visit.

Lori walked into the elevator and noticed that her heart was pounding again. What does someone say to a person who tried killing herself? Should she say something like: "Did you really want to die that badly?" Or: "Are you upset that you woke up?" The question she really wanted to ask was: "Why did you do it?"

Lori passed the nurses' station and stopped to find out the way to Hannah's room. She turned left, following the nurse's directions. Then she saw it. Room 507. She took a deep breath and opened the door.

There was Hannah lying on the bed with an IV line pumping into her. She looked pale, but other than that, relatively normal. Lori's parents were in the room, too.

"Hi, Hannah!" Lori tried to sound cheerful.

"Lori, you didn't have to come!" Hannah said, sounding embarrassed.

"Hi, Lori! Sorry I didn't get to see you last night. You left too quickly," Sam called out.

"Hi, Dad!"

There was an awkward silence.

"I think that Dad and I are going to go out and get some breakfast," Elaine said quickly. "Hannah, do you want me to bring anything back for you?"

"Not right now, thanks."

Lori's mom and dad left, leaving Lori alone with Hannah.

Lori sat down beside Hannah's bed.

"Lori," Hannah said, hesitating slightly "It means a lot to me that you came."

"Well, don't do this again to get me back here, okay? You had me really scared. Next time just call, and I'd love to come visit!"

"Sorry. I guess I did something really stupid."

Lori wanted to say, *You sure did!* But instead she said, "No, Hannah, don't say that!" which didn't make too much sense, either.

"No, I really did. I was feeling so great after the Nobel week…" Her voice trailed off.

"So what happened?" Lori spoke before she could catch herself.

"I was feeling so great that I decided to stop taking my medication."

"Your medication for…" Lori paused, trying to remember what Hannah was taking medication for, "…depression?"

"Well, that, and you know, for my bipolar stuff."

Lori jolted upright in her seat. "You…you have bipolar?"

"You don't know that?" Hannah sounded genuinely shocked.

"How would I know?" Lori tried to sound nonchalant. Of course, Hannah had bipolar disorder. It seemed so obvious in retrospect. How had she not known?

"I assumed Mom and Dad told you."

"How long have you known you had bipolar?"

"I had my first episode when I was sixteen. Remember when I returned from college and I was depressed?"

How could Lori have forgotten that?

"But I wasn't diagnosed until I was twenty-two. Over the years, I've tried different medications, been to numerous psychiatrists and psychologists, and been in all sorts of therapy. Over the past few years, I was doing really well. My last full-blown episode was during the twins' first birthday celebration. I'm sure you remember how Mom and Dad had to cancel their trip to you. Since then, I've been stable.

"Things had gone so well in Stockholm and I just felt so great that I wanted to try life off of medication again. I guess in the back of my mind, I sort of missed the mania episodes, too. I've done some of my best research when I was in a manic state. I had this weird urge to produce some great science work again. I thought maybe the depression was worth enduring to experience the mania…" Hannah's voice trailed off.

"It seems crazy when I describe it. Anyway, it was the dumbest thing I could have done. I went into a terrible depression. It's so hard to explain. I just felt hopeless and wanted to end it all. It was worse than ever. It was like I came crashing down from the sky."

Lori stumbled on her words. "Oh…oh…" She was a little angry at Hannah that she had never shared any of this with her, and a little angry at herself that she hadn't realized this on her own. Although she must have known it deep down. "So now what?"

"My psychiatrist is helping me. I guess I won't ever go off the medication again." Hannah sighed.

"Does that upset you?"

"It is a little depressing."

Lori sat there not knowing what to say. The shock was slowly wearing off. She couldn't decide if it was a big deal that Hannah had been diagnosed as having bipolar all these years and she hadn't known. Bipolar is a serious psychiatric disorder. A life-altering disorder. A genetic disorder. A disorder that affects jobs and relationships. Lori would have been much more sensitive to Hannah's needs if she had known. Or maybe she wouldn't have been. Who knew?

And what about the increased risks of her own children developing a similar sickness? With Matthew similar to Hannah in many ways, did that put him at an increased risk of developing a mood disorder? Was there any way to prevent it? Only one more issue to worry about.

Dr. Wilson looked at Lori. "Just another little twist to the story. So how is Hannah doing now?"

"She's home from the hospital and supposedly going back to work in a week or so. She was really lucky the neighbor found her when she did. If she wouldn't have been found for a few more hours, the implications would have been far more serious."

"So do you feel better now about all the times Hannah seemed to ruin things for you?"

"I'm not sure. I've thought about it a lot this past week. I'm still confused. I don't understand why I didn't realize that she had a major psychiatric disorder on my own." Lori shook her head back and forth.

"You know, I was thinking the same thing. Looking back, the clues seem obvious. The pattern of dysfunctional episodes should have been an indication of something."

Lori shrugged and raised her eyebrows. "I guess I really knew it deep down, but it was easier to blame her when I didn't have to admit that she was truly suffering herself. It was that defense to protect the guilt, like you've been helping me appreciate." Lori paused again and then she added, "I had one more interesting conversation with her, but I know that our time is up. Can we finish this conversation next week?"

"Sounds good to me."

CHAPTER 28

LORI ENTERED THE OFFICE.

"Hi, Lori."

"Hello."

"I hope this was a calmer week."

Lori smiled. "Yes, much calmer. Hannah is back at work. My mom and dad are back home."

"And your life?"

"Everything is relatively calm, too. Emma is really enjoying the art lessons. It seems like it was a good decision. I had some stressful interactions with David, but nothing major. I think I was just exhausted, emotionally and physically. Hopefully, we're back to normal life now. Whatever normal is!"

"So what was that other conversation you had with Hannah during your visit?"

"I stayed in the hospital for most of that day. I had a flight back early the next morning. At one point, my mom had gone out to pick up dinner, and my dad had gone to shower at the hotel. Yes, they finally checked into a hotel. I was sitting with Hannah. As we were talking, we began reminiscing about different childhood memories. We were laughing and joking. I was having fun. Suddenly, Hannah said something that caught me off guard."

"You know, Lori," Hannah's tone dropped. "My whole life, I

was so jealous of you."

"Jealous — of me? What are you talking about?" Lori didn't know where this conversation was going.

"Yeah. I was so jealous of your relationship with Mom and Dad." Hannah looked away. She seemed to have tears in her eyes.

"What are you saying? My whole life I've been so jealous of *you*! Of your relationship with Mom and Dad!"

"No, no. Mom and Dad treated you so normally. They let you do normal things, have normal friends. I was always so trapped. I had this talent that I had to live up to. I had these expectations. I always had to be studying, learning, developing my skills. I always had to talk to adults, show off my skills. I couldn't ever just play. Mom and Dad would laugh with you, play with you, take you and your friends to fun places. I never had any of that! I just wanted to be you.

"Mom and Dad were so strict with me. They had to be in-volved in every decision that I made. They let you be so free. They respected you as a person so much more than me. When you became a teenager, they'd even ask advice from you. That would drive me the craziest. Why wouldn't they trust my opin-ion? Why didn't they want to know what I thought?" Hannah blew her nose.

"Hannah, it's crazy that you're saying that. Do you know how much I always dreamed that I could be you? You were the highlight of their lives, the reason for their existence. I was a meaningless blob compared to you. When company came, they'd have you show off your talents, while I'd be ignored like a painting on the wall. Dad's face would light up when he talk-ed about math with you. It would give him renewed energy. He never knew what to talk to me about. All Mom and Dad's resources went to you; all their time and energy were devoted to helping you.

"Sometimes, I felt that if I would've dropped dead, they wouldn't have even noticed." Now Lori was blowing her nose.

Hannah was staring at Lori. "Do you mean that? Or are you just saying it to make me feel better?"

Lori's brain could not catch up with all it had to absorb. First, she'd heard the news that Hannah was bipolar all these years without her knowing. Now, she was hearing that Hannah had been jealous of her all these years.

Hannah continued, "Mom always wanted you to help her shop. She'd laugh if I tried to give her my opinion. Both Mom and Dad always seemed to enjoy being with you. When they were with me, it always seemed like a chore, like a task they had to do." Hannah sniffled. Lori blew her nose.

"I always had this huge pressure on my head," Hannah continued. "I knew I had these amazing abilities — and I'd have to use them to save the world. If I didn't, my life was wasted. I could never relax, do something fun. You, on the other hand, always seemed to be living fun. Everything that you did was exciting. And no one ever stopped you. Mom and Dad would laugh about all your escapades when you weren't listening. They thought you were the cutest kid..."

Hannah wiped her eyes. "Oh, what's the use? Why am I saying all this? I'm just getting myself all worked up and making you feel bad. I didn't want to do this. I really wanted to just enjoy my time with you." Hannah lay back down on her pillow and turned her head away.

Lori was in shock. But she had to stay in control. She was the psychologist by training. She had to muster all the strength she had to turn this into a positive experience. "Hannah, I'm so happy you're sharing all this with me. I really am!" She swallowed hard. "Do you know how strange it is to hear you say this? I've been going to therapy, too, to help me deal with all my resentments. I've spent my life brooding over the fact that Mom and Dad love you more, that they would've been happier if I'd never been born and they could just dedicate their time to you. Isn't it crazy how we each spent our lives wishing we could be each other?"

Hannah stared at Lori. Her eyes were filled with tears that were about to brim over. Lori reached out for Hannah's hand, and Hannah took it. They sat there in silence for a moment.

"Lori?" Hannah's voice was quiet. "I really admire you."

"Thanks, Hannah. I have to say, it's mutual. With everything you've been through, you've persevered. No matter how difficult all those expectations were, you lived up to them. You have changed mankind. How many people can say that?"

Hannah smiled. "You're an awesome sister." She breathed in deeply. "I'm tired."

"Why don't you take a nap? I'll check if Mom's back with the food."

"Will you come back before you leave?"

"Of course."

Lori looked at Dr. Wilson. "So what do you think of that? Isn't it strange when you think you know everything, you think everything is so obvious, and then you hear the other person's side…"

Dr. Wilson looked back at Lori. "What a story." He picked up a tissue and blew his nose.

"Are you getting emotional?" Lori asked incredulously.

"No, no, just a cold." Dr. Wilson smiled and gave Lori a wink.

No one said anything until Dr. Wilson broke the silence. "So how was the rest of the trip?"

"My mom brought back dinner. We all ate together. I said good-bye to everyone and caught an early flight out the next morning."

Dr. Wilson was about to say something when Lori interjected, "Oh, and there's something else I have to show you. With all the craziness with Hannah, I completely forgot about this." She rummaged through her purse. "You'll never believe this, either. I got it in the mail the day that Hannah tried to kill herself." She continued searching until she pulled out an envelope and handed it to Dr. Wilson. "Check this out."

Dr. Wilson looked down, not sure what to expect. He took the envelope and opened it.

> Dear Lori,
>
> Sorry about our conversation on our walk in Stockholm. It's been bothering me since then. I just wish that if you read my diary, you would have kept reading. I copied a later entry that I thought you would appreciate reading. I hope this helps you. I enjoyed our trip immensely. It meant a lot to Dad and me that you came and brought David, Emma, and Matthew.
>
> Love,
> Mom

Dr. Wilson turned the page and continued reading.

Today Lori turned seven months old. She is the cutest, happiest baby I have ever seen. I'm totally in love with her. It's strange. I never felt this way with Hannah. Hannah was always such a difficult child. I love Hannah more than anything, but in a different way. I can't believe we were ever concerned about having another child. Lori is bringing us so much joy in a new way. I can tell that she will be such a great balance to our lives. We are so lucky to have her.

Dr. Wilson looked up. "Wait, now I need time to process all this." He looked at Lori in wonder.

"Yeah, it's interesting how things work out."

"So what are you doing with all this information?"

"I don't know. I just keep trying to think about what I can do to try to prevent this kind of thing from happening to Emma and Matthew."

"Did you come up with any of your usual great ideas?"

Lori grinned. "Not yet. But I'll keep thinking."

"Knowing your track record, I know you won't stop until you do."

"Anyway, Dr. Wilson, I want to thank you profusely. You gave me the courage to deal with all my emotions, to understand myself, to go to Stockholm, to bring up these difficult subjects with my family members in a calm and positive way…"

"Lori, you're an inspiration in all your life endeavors. I just feel lucky that you let me help you."

Lori sat back and sighed deeply. "Life is strange."

Dr. Wilson also sighed. "I agree."

CHAPTER 29

ORI WAS SITTING IN HER office at the clinic. It was a Tuesday morning in February, two months since the Nobel Prize ceremonies and about eight months since she had first met Allison. She had just had a canceled session and had some free time for the first time in a while. There was something she really wanted to do. She was not going to push it off any longer.

She rummaged through her files until she found Allison's chart. She pulled it out and opened it up. Looking through it, she found what she wanted. Breathing in deeply, she lifted the phone off the receiver. Then she dialed Allison's home number. Lori waited as the phone rang, almost hoping no one would answer. Once, twice, three times. And then, she heard the distinct click of the phone being answered.

"Hello?"

The voice on the other end sounded like Katie. Lori tried to stay calm. Was Katie going to slam the phone down when Lori announced who she was? "Hi! This is Lori Green from Rainbow Clinic."

"Lori? Yes, what can I do for you?" Katie's voice was cold but she had not hung up.

Lori suddenly felt stuck. Should she ask about Allison first or apologize first? There was a nagging fear hanging over her that Allison had died, and that would make this conversation a lot more difficult. How could she apologize without knowing if Allison was alive? On the other hand, how could she talk to Katie before she apologized?

"Hello?" Katie repeated impatiently.

Lori was taking too long. "Katie, I'm calling because I wanted to apologize for the way I handled our last meeting when you were at the clinic. I've thought about you often since then. I'm really sorry that I seemed to blame you for Allison's difficulties. That must have been awful." There. She had done it. She had said the words she'd been practicing for months. How would Katie react?

Katie was silent for a long moment. And then, "Yes, you did say some rotten things. But I've gotten past it."

Well, that was not exactly the warm reaction Lori was hoping to hear, but she would take it. Now for the next question. "I've thought about Allison often, too. How is she doing?"

"Allison?" Katie responded.

Lori's heart skipped a beat. *Just answer already! Is she alive or not?*

"Allison is doing…okay."

Lori released the breath she hadn't realized she had been holding. "I'm happy to hear that." She tried to keep her tone calm.

"Yes, we've had some real scares in the past few months, but it seems that Allison is hanging on. It was pretty awful after we left your clinic." Katie's voice grew louder as she seemed to be warming up.

"Really?" Lori was trying to comment as little as possible, hoping Katie would share more this way.

"Yeah. Allison was so upset that I pulled her out of Rainbow Clinic that she completely shut down. I think she was trying to punish me. In any case, she stopped eating entirely. When we checked her into the children's hospital the next week, she was so close to dying. And even then, the doctors had to put her arms in restraints to keep a nasogastric tube in her. It was terrible." Katie's voice shuddered as she spoke. "Even worse than that, my relationship with her was in a terrible state. At one point, she refused to talk to me and ignored me for at least a week."

Again, Lori kept her comments to a minimum. "Really?"

"But then the tide began to turn, just ever so slightly."

"What do you mean?"

"Allison began to make real progress in therapy for the first time ever."

Lori waited for Katie to elaborate, but Katie said nothing. Finally, Lori asked the obvious question. "How did that happen?"

"Well, as angry as I was with you for the way that you handled everything, the last session that you had with Allison was really what started things." Lori smiled to herself knowingly. So she had done something positive, after all. Now Katie would thank her. "But not in the way that you would think," she added.

Lori stopped smiling. "Can you explain?"

"Okay. You know, I did not appreciate the way you spoke to me that day. But what bothered me the most was how you were so sure you had everything figured out that you wouldn't stop and listen to me. I was trying to tell you something, but you never got it."

Lori's mind raced. She tried to replay the conversation in her head. What could she have missed? What was Katie referring to?

"When I told you that Allison was lying, I meant it. Allison had a brother, Will, but he was not diagnosed with ODD when he was in second grade. He died when he was in second grade." Katie stopped and Lori tried to digest what she had just heard. Allison did not have a brother living in a home? Lori couldn't process everything that Katie was saying.

"I'm...I'm terribly sorry. That's awful. Had he been sick?"

"You're right; it was horrible. I wouldn't wish it on my worst enemy. And no, he was not sick. It was the day before Christmas and I was at the mall with him doing some last-minute shopping. Suddenly, he dropped to the floor... He never woke up... They administered CPR the whole way to the hospital, but he was DOA... The autopsy report said that he had a genetic heart defect." Katie's voice had a hollow ring to it.

"So the brother Allison had been talking about has not been alive all these years?" Did Allison have some other undiagnosed mental disorder? This story was becoming bizarre. In truth, a lot of the details of Allison's story had seemed very odd. Especially that Allison had not seen her brother since he had been eight! Why hadn't Lori thought of it then?

"Here's the crazy part. Allison was four at the time that Will died. We didn't know how to tell her that he was dead, so we told her that Will had gone to a better place. A place where he wouldn't have any more sad or bad times. We did not take Allison to the funeral. And then, we never talked about Will. My husband couldn't and I didn't want to.

"Allison, in her interesting mind, never let herself believe that the older brother whom she adored had died. We think she knew deep down, but she concocted all kinds of crazy ideas to convince herself that he could still be alive. He'd been a somewhat difficult child, always having terrible tantrums. Allison thought that we sent him away to help with his behavior — that was the 'better place' that we had told her about.

"As Allison grew older, she read up about behavior disorders and decided that Will had a terrible case of ODD. She believed that we had placed him in an institution. Whenever we didn't tell her where we were going, she would imagine that we were going to visit Will. She thought that we were spending all our extra money on his treatment. She found all these 'clues' to prove that her ideas were correct."

Katie swallowed. "Of course, Allison never told us what she was thinking because Will was a totally taboo topic in our house. We never imagined that she didn't realize that he had died. We never realized how much was going on in her little brain all those years. Allison also had a secret fear that if she misbehaved, she would be sent to 'that place,' too."

Lori was trying to stay composed. The story kept getting crazier. Allison hadn't had a brother. Katie had spoken literally when she said that Allison was lying. Lori had been so convinced that Katie had "neglected" Allison that she'd never even given Katie a chance to speak.

"Anyway, all of this has slowly been coming out during therapy. When we were at our lowest point — with Allison lying in the hospital, seeming intent on dying, with our only chance of keeping her alive by keeping her arms in restraints and a tube pumping calories into her body, with the added stress of my marriage in absolute tatters — I decided to put myself in therapy. I just couldn't cope anymore. While in therapy, I began to deal with the grief I had never overcome after Will had died. I've come to recognize that in my grief, I'd totally shut myself off from Allison, too. I was just so scared that something would happen to her, that she would just drop dead one day, that I never wanted to become too attached. I always kept myself distant..."

Katie sniffled a couple of times. "Also, I kept reverting to that bizarre session she had with you. At first, I was sure she had intentionally lied to you for some strange reason that I could not figure out. I tried to block it out of my mind and just deal with the desperate state Allison was in. I never brought it up with her, never told Tom. But I couldn't block it out for long. And as I thought about it more and more, I began to wonder if she could have really believed what she told you. Maybe she really believed Will was alive...

"I met with the therapist and reviewed all the information. The therapist said that we'd have to tell Allison the story of Will's death — tell her about the funeral, tell her about our feelings — and not leave anything out. We'd have to say everything explicitly, no matter how hard it would be. He offered to be there as a mediator if we chose to talk about it during therapy. That sounded like a good idea to me, but I didn't know how Tom would take it. Surprisingly, he thought it was a great idea.

"The first session in which Tom and I had to talk about Will's death, and say those words out loud...was horribly painful. Painful for Tom and me, and painful for Allison. At first, she didn't believe us. Then slowly, it all came out. All the years of her believing that he was still alive. All the rationalizations her mind formed to convince herself that it was true. All the mistakes we made in never allowing Will's name to be mentioned. You know, we really thought we were helping Allison, making the house a happier place by not talking about him...

"Anyway, the therapist suggested we all take a trip to Will's grave. We did that. And we all started the grieving process from scratch. Tom and I have also come to recognize that in our failure to grieve, we actually allowed ourselves to be preoccupied with thoughts of Will. We hardly had room in our world for Allison. It's been a difficult process, but we're all learning... "

"As all of us are, Katie," Lori interjected. "As all of us are."

"We've also learned that Allison has an unusual gift for writing poetry. This wonderful therapist has been working with her and using Allison's ability to communicate through poetry to help her share all the bottled-up thoughts that she has such a difficult time expressing."

Katie sighed deeply. "Well, that's the short story. But believe me, this was not the cure-all. Allison has her ups and downs. She was home for a month, but she's back in the hospital. We're hopeful that she will beat this disease. But the fear of the what-ifs doesn't let me sleep at night. It's so horrible to watch your child starve herself to death, and you can't do anything to stop it. It feels like the thing you want most in the world is right in front of you, but there's a glass wall surrounding it and nothing you do can break through the wall. You only have a limited time to get it out; otherwise it'll self-destruct. And all you can do is stare through the glass."

Katie's voice faltered again and she sniffed, trying to maintain her composure. "I'm trying so hard to hold on to her. I don't want her to die." The word "die" escaped from her mouth like a moan. The pain Katie was experiencing was so raw and so palpable, Lori had to bite her lips to avert sobs from exploding out of her own mouth. She almost wanted to slam down the phone and pretend she had never heard Katie's story. Just make it fade from her memory like a bad dream.

Katie continued, "My only solace is that I've developed a real relationship with Allison in a way I missed out on all these years. Suddenly, I feel so close to her. I only wish it hadn't taken this horrible disease to pull us together."

Lori didn't say a word. Katie was in another world, not seeming to notice if she was there or not.

Katie sighed again. "As hard as this was for me, I swore to Allison that no matter what, I will never force her to undergo any treatments that she does not agree to. She's requested no feeding tube, and I will abide by her wishes. I'm trying my best to respect her rights, even if that means having to let her go. Surprisingly, giving her this assurance has seemed to free her to get better. Giving her back that control has helped give her strength to fight harder. I am holding on to my hope... Holding on..."

"What a story," said Lori. "I apologize again for jumping to conclusions. Now I understand why you were so upset."

"Anyway, I've been rambling and rambling. I appreciate that you called, and I'll tell Allison that you asked about her."

"Yes, please do that. And please stay in touch." Lori had many more questions, but she didn't feel comfortable pushing Katie any further.

"Okay. Goodbye!"

Lori heard the abrupt click of the phone as Katie hung up. She slowly put her own phone back in its place and started straightening the papers scattered across her desk. If she thought this phone call would put an end to her compulsive checking of obituaries, she was wrong. It would only increase her urge to check.

Thoughts rambled and roared through her mind. Just when you thought you had everything all figured out, you realized you were actually clueless.

EPILOGUE

I
T WAS A MARVELOUS SPRING Sunday afternoon. Lori was sitting at the park, watching Emma and Matthew running around, playing, climbing, and laughing. She turned her face toward the sun, enjoying its warmth, and closed her eyes and let her thoughts wander.

The sound of her ringing cell phone jolted her back to reality. She glanced down at the caller ID. It was Hannah. Lori wondered what was up.

"Hello?"

"Hi, Lori. It's Hannah."

"Hi, Hannah. How are you?"

"I'm good. I just wanted to share some news with you."

"What is it?"

"I'm going to be accepting a new position. I'm really excited about it. The college is giving me an impressive research facility and a great group of graduate fellows to work for me. And a great salary."

"Really? That sounds wonderful."

"Wait — I didn't tell you the best part."

"Yes?" Lori wondered what it could be.

"I'm going to be at Princeton, which, I believe, is a thirty-minute drive from your home."

"Hannah, that's so exciting!" Lori replied a little too quickly. Her first thoughts were of worry. She hoped Hannah wouldn't be too needy, hoped they could maintain their new friendship — and that being closer wouldn't ruin things.

"I'm excited about being nearer to you, too," continued Hannah. "And especially about spending more time with Emma and Matthew. They're growing up so fast. I don't want to miss this time in their lives. I was even thinking that Matthew could come to my lab sometimes and I can do experiments with him. I can take both of them on outings. I can babysit for you guys, if you ever want to get away..."

"That sounds great. I didn't even know you were considering this." As Hannah's words sank in, Lori's mind began to race, as she processed the news and got used to the idea. Maybe this would be a good thing. Or even a very good thing. Half an hour away gave them some distance, while they were still close enough that they could spend more time together.

"I didn't want to tell you until I was sure. I didn't want to ruin anything."

"Have you talked to Mom and Dad about it?"

"Yes, they're very happy about it."

Hannah and Lori continued talking for a while longer. Then Lori hung up the phone and placed it back in her purse. A smile slowly spread across her face. She breathed in the fresh air and took in the scene around her. The sky was bright blue. The air smelled delicious. Flowers were budding all around. Happy laughter filled the air.

Life was beautiful.

For the moment, at least.

CPSIA information can be obtained
at www.ICGtesting.com
Printed in the USA
LVHW022346220721
693426LV00011B/761